A Fox for Faith

Love will OUT #4

D.E. Haggerty

Also By D.E. Haggerty

A Hero for Hailey
A Protector for Phoebe
A Soldier for Suzie
A Christmas for Chrissie
A Valentine for Valerie
A Love for Lexi
My Forever Love
Forever For You
Just For Forever
Stay For Forever
Only Forever
Meet Disaster
Meet Not
Meet Dare
Meet Hate
Bragg's Truth
Bragg's Love
Perfect Bragg
About Face
At Arm's Length

Hands Off
Knee Deep
Molly's Misadventures

Chapter 1

Parenting was much easier when I was hypothetically raising my non-existent son.

"I DON'T WANT TO GO," Ollie says in that whiny voice teenagers around the world have perfected.

I nearly snap at him. Oh boy, do I want to snap at him. But a good mother does not snap at her son, and I do try to be a good mother. Instead, I take a deep breath and find my inner calm before responding.

"And I didn't want to give up all my friends and my job to move to Milwaukee, but here we are." I guess I didn't find my inner calm after all.

Ollie comes to a screeching halt. Or as much of a screeching halt as a lanky, hasn't grown into his long limbs yet, fifteen-year-old can come to. "I'm sorry, Ma. I didn't mean for you to lose everything and move us here. I was only trying to help."

Sigh. Oliver Benjamin Bakker is always 'only trying to help'. But how can I berate him for having the biggest heart in the world? I can't, is how. I don't understand how I and my jerk of an ex-husband, Silas, created the most perfect creature in the world, which is exactly what this boy with puppy dog brown eyes, shaggy brown hair, and freckles galore is, but we did.

"Stop it, Ma."

"Stop what?" What am I doing wrong now?

He bumps my shoulder. "You know what. The whole mushy look you get on your face right before you try to hug me to death."

"Me? Hug you to death?" I mock before I throw my arms around him and try to do that very thing he hates.

"Ma, we're in public." He may complain, but he does wrap his arms around me and squeezes me back. My boy may be fifteen, but he's not afraid to show his mom a little love. This right here is why I work two jobs and run around playing taxi for him.

"Can we go inside now?"

"I thought you didn't want to go," I tease as I release him from my hug of death.

He scoffs. "Even seeing your boss and all his weirdo friends is better than getting mauled to death in a parking lot."

To say my son is not a fan of my boss is a vast understatement. It's a shame since my boss at McGraw's Pub, where I'm currently working as a cleaner, is a sweetheart. Unfortunately, he calls all the women in his life darling, which my boy takes offense to. Ollie's convinced my boss, aka Pops, is hitting on me all the time. As if I have time for a relationship.

"You ready?" I ask as I grasp the handle to the door of the pub.

The pub is closed to the public tonight so we can celebrate Suzie and Grayson's surprise wedding. Suzie is the best friend of Pops' daughter, Hailey. She and Grayson eloped this weekend to Las Vegas. Actually, Suzie didn't know what Grayson had planned. The two weren't engaged as far as I know, but he swept her off to Vegas for Labor Day weekend where he ambushed her with a completely planned wedding. Only a former soldier could possibly plan and execute a romantic elopement without crazy girl Suzie catching on.

"You're doing it again," Ollie whines.

"What?"

"Getting the mushy look on your face. Do you need another hug?" he asks despite his nose scrunching in distaste. I should probably hug him to tease him. Lucky for him, there's no time as some of Suzie's friends have arrived and are waiting to enter behind us.

"Hi, Faith!" Phoebe smiles in greeting. As usual, the woman looks like she just stepped off the runway in Paris. You would never guess she's a private investigator at the PI firm Hailey and Suzie own together. I look at her wrap dress and high heels, and then down at the black slacks and blouse I'm wearing. I fiddle with the hem of my blouse. It's one of my nicest, satin with a plunging neckline, but should I have worn a skirt?

"I love this shirt." Phoebe fingers the sleeve of my blouse. "It looks great on your figure. I can't wear a plunging neckline without worrying about giving people an unintended peep show." She motions to her more than abundant breasts. Lucky her. I was apparently last in line when they were handing out curves.

Her fiancé, Ryker, puts his arm around her shoulders and tugs her near. "You look beautiful, Princess," he whispers before kissing her forehead. She practically melts into his side.

It's not hard to imagine Ryker is a big, badass bounty hunter. He's at least six and a half feet tall and is built like a Mack truck. His entire body telegraphs menace. If it weren't for the soft looks he shares with Phoebe, I'd be more than a little apprehensive of the man.

Behind them, Ollie feigns gagging at their display of affection. I roll my eyes at him, but secretly I'm relieved he's not obsessed with girls yet. I know the phase will come when girls and teenage hormones will overtake him. And I'm not looking forward to the day.

"Pops is going to love this top," Phoebe says with a wink as she strolls past us into the pub.

I ignore her comment. Pops' daughter and all her friends have been pushing Pops and me together since my first day of work cleaning at the pub. No thanks. One teenage boy at a time is enough for me. Never mind how my skin erupts in goosebumps every time his bright blue eyes gaze at me.

"Come on." I motion for Ollie to proceed me into the pub. "Let's get this over with."

Although we're one of the last to arrive, the pub isn't overly crowded when we walk in. Suzie and Grayson are standing in the middle of the room next to a table of gifts. Two older couples are standing with them. This must be the parents.

Judging by the screeching, someone's mom is not happy they eloped.

At a table to the right, Suzie's uncles are congregating. Actually, Lenny, Barney, Wally, and Sid aren't her uncles. In fact, they're no one's uncles as far as I can figure. From what I've gathered, the four men are former Army buddies of Pops who helped raise Hailey after her mom took off.

Pops is in his usual position behind the bar. He looks up as we walk in and aims a smile our way. "Spitfire, you made it."

I nearly turn into a puddle of goo when he calls me spitfire. I know it's stupid. I'm a forty-five-year old woman, I shouldn't be going all gooey over a man calling me spitfire – especially not my boss. But he calls every other woman in the world darling. Not me. For me, he has a special nickname. Having a man who looks like Pops direct his attention my way causes parts of my body I thought had died off from lack of attention to wake up.

If you look silver fox up in the dictionary, you'll find a picture of Pops. His hair may be silver, but it looks lush and soft. I can't help but wonder what it would feel like if I ran my hands through it. His gray-tinged beard makes him look distinguished even in his standard uniform of jeans and a t-shirt with the logo for McGraw's Pub on it. The t-shirt is stretched to the max over his shoulders and biceps. He may be in his mid-fifties, but he hasn't let his tall physique go. My fingers itch to touch those hard muscles. But it's his eyes that ensnare me. They're bright blue and when he looks at you, you feel like you're the only person in the world who exists for him.

I wave. "Hi!" Great. I sound like a total dork.

"Faith!" Suzie calls and draws my attention away from the silver fox.

The red-headed firecracker rushes to me and throws her arms around me. Or, I should say, she tries to throw her arms around me. I may not be tall at five-six, but Suzie barely passes the five-foot mark. I'm not sure why she's clinging to me, though, it's not like we're close friends.

"Save me," she whispers.

"In-law or parents?" I ask. I have some experience with judgmental in-laws. According to them, it's all my fault Silas left me and my son. As if there's ever an excuse to leave your child.

"Parents," Suzie whispers. "My in-laws are the bomb."

"Lucky you," I mutter before clearing my throat. "I have a present for you." And the dorkiness continues. Of course, I have a present for her. It's her party.

"Grayson," Suzie shouts and waves her brand-new husband over. "Come here."

He grins at the two sets of parents before sauntering our way. He may only be an inch or two taller than me, but his broad physique screams soldier who can take care of business.

"Now I know where your crazy comes from," he says as he takes Suzie's hand in his.

She huffs. "Who are you calling crazy?"

Grayson opens his mouth, but I lift the gift bag and shove it in their faces before he can insert his foot. "Happy marriage!"

Suzie bounces on her toes and snatches the bag from me. "Thank you!"

"It's no big deal."

Despite working two jobs, I'm not exactly flush with cash. Things would be much easier if I could find a job as a paralegal. But law firms do background checks on their employees, and I can't chance my name popping up on someone's computer. Thus, a cleaning job and a filing job. Together I'm earning barely half of what my previous paralegal position paid.

Suzie removes the gift from the bag and her eyes widen. "These are way cool. Thank you!" She shoves the mugs at Grayson and hugs me again.

I pat her back. "Um, you're welcome."

When she releases me, it's Grayson's turn. "Awesome gift, Faith. Thanks."

"It's nothing." I had two beer mugs engraved with the logo of Suzie's microbrewery – Shorty's Brewing Sensation. On top of owning the private investigator business with Hailey, Suzie brews beer. In fact, her beer is becoming quite popular with the local bars.

"Oh wow." Hailey joins us and takes one of the mugs from Suzie's hands. "These are cool. I wish I had thought of this."

Hailey's husband, Aiden, steps up behind her. "You want me to take our gift back?"

Hailey and Aiden look like they stepped off the pages of a high school yearbook. He's the quintessential quarterback with his tall, fit body. While Hailey resembles the head cheerleader with her long, dancer body. Looks can be deceiving, though. He's now a police detective, she's a private investigator. From what I hear, they re-connected while Hailey was on a case and Aiden caught her snooping where she shouldn't have been.

Suzie slaps Aiden's chest. "No take backs, mister."

I try to tamp down my jealousy as I watch the friends interact. It's not their fault I had to abandon my friends when Ollie and I fled to Milwaukee. The police advised I cut all contact with them after we settled in, and, except for my best friend Valerie who I keep in touch with via social media, I've been a good girl and listened to their advice. I can only hope the people Ollie pissed off aren't sophisticated enough to hack into my social media accounts.

I excuse myself and head toward the restrooms. I need a moment to myself before I let my jealousy consume me. When I exit the restroom, Pops is waiting on me.

He steps toward me with a predatory gleam in his eyes, and I freeze. His hand lifts, and he tucks a strand of my hair behind my ear. I inhale and his crispy, woodsy scent fills my lungs. I want to roll around in it.

"Thanks for coming, Spitfire."

His breath on my skin causes my hormones to go wild. Calm down, hormones. I'm not a lovesick teenager. My hormones don't care. My belly warms, and my breasts swell. Uh oh. Danger. I step back, but there's nowhere to go. I'm cornered in the hallway with my back up against the wall – literally.

"Of course, we came, Pops," I manage to say without sounding too breathy.

He growls. "You don't call me Pops."

I wrinkle my brow in confusion. "But everyone calls you Pops." Oh shit. I slap my palm against my forehead when

I realize what I've done wrong. He's my boss. Of course, I shouldn't act familiar with him. "I'm sorry, Mr. McGraw."

His growl intensifies, and he takes a step closer until his chest is barely an inch from mine. My fingers itch to touch him, and I'm tempted to arch my back and rub my breasts against him. What is wrong with me? I'm not a hussy. Hell, since my ex Silas left, I've barely dated let alone touched a man. Why is this one causing me to act like someone I am most definitely not?

"I am not Mr. McGraw or Pops to you. You call me Max."

"M-m-max?" I hate how my voice stutters, but I can't catch my breath when he's this close.

"Or darling or sweetheart or baby. I'll answer to any of those names as long as you're the one doing the calling."

My eyes widen. "I thought we agreed we weren't going to date." Because, despite what I told Ollie, Pops has asked me out. I'm not exactly lying to my son. Asking someone out is not the same thing as hitting on them. I am a master at treading a fine line between the truth and a lie.

It's a non-issue anyway. I'm not stupid. I'm not dating my boss. Besides, I'm in Milwaukee temporarily.

"Fair warning. I'm done waiting."

"Ma!" Ollie shouts, and I tear my eyes away from Max's blue gaze. "What are you doing?"

Lord save me from fifteen-year-old sons. "I'm fine. I'll be there in a minute."

He glares at Max who returns his glare with one of his own. While he's distracted, I shove him and catch him enough off guard that I'm able to duck under his arm.

"I'm ready to go," I tell Ollie, although we arrived less than an hour ago.

Before I can make my escape, Max yells, "See you tomorrow, Spitfire."

As if I need the reminder.

Chapter 2

I love it when I find myself screaming 'stop screaming' at my kid.

"Come on, Ollie. Get a move on. I'm going to be late to work."

And after Monday night, I do not want to be late. Late means I'll end up seeing Pops way more than I want to. And now I'm lying to myself over a man. I promised myself I'd never lie to myself about a man again after Silas the no-good-doer. And yet here I am. One heated look from my boss and I dissolve into a puddle of goo. Not good.

Ollie rushes out of his room. His hair is sticking straight up, his t-shirt is untucked, and he's only wearing one sock. *Take a breath, Faith. This is not the end of the world.*

"You're missing a sock, and I think you're wearing your pajama top," I tell him as I point to his t-shirt which says *If sleeping, do not disturb.*

Ollie looks down at his shirt. "Oh yeah. BRB."

I ignore the use of a stupid acronym because I learned long ago as a mom to choose my battles. "Don't forget your backpack."

Ollie skids to a halt. "Can you look for my algebra book? I think it's in the living room somewhere."

How this kid manages to get good grades is beyond me. I huff and march to the living room to search for his book. It's nowhere in sight, but from experience, I know where to look. "Aha!" I raise my arm in victory when I find the book tucked between the armrest and the cushion.

I hand my boy his book when he returns, this time wearing a long-sleeve black t-shirt and two socks. I'm not sure they match, but I am sure I don't care. "Let's go."

"I haven't had breakfast yet," he whines.

I can't deny my kid breakfast, but I'm no dummy either. I hand him the bacon and cheese bagel I made him. "You can eat on the way to school."

Somehow, I manage to get Ollie offloaded at his school, but by the time I arrive at McGraw's Pub for work, I'm nearly an hour late. Maybe if I work my butt off, I can get all the cleaning done before the pub opens for lunch. My hopes are dashed when I walk inside. This is going to be a back-breaking day. Oh goodie. I put my hair up in a knot and get to work.

I mop, wipe down tables, and scrub stains like a madwoman. I'm sweating through my t-shirt by the time I'm nearly finished. And – bonus! – I've managed to avoid Pops all morning. He doesn't usually come down from his apartment above the pub until after nine and then he stays in his office doing paperwork, but we do usually take a coffee break together. Today, though, he hasn't emerged from his office all morning.

My stomach sours at the thought. Maybe he's given up on me already. Ugh! I want him to give up on me, remember? I tell my stomach. We don't have room in our life for a man, especially one who's still in love with his ex-wife. At the reminder of the ex-wife, the sour in my stomach changes to an ache.

Pops hasn't mentioned one word about his ex, but Hailey filled in the blanks for me. Apparently, her dad hasn't been in a relationship since her mom left. I can read between the lines. He's still totally in love with his wife. Why else would he be single? The man is gorgeous, owns his own business, and for all intents and purposes seems like a good guy. A woman would have snapped him up by now if he was open to a relationship.

Someone touches my shoulder, and I twirl around with my hand curled in a fist. Pops raises his hands and takes a step back. I narrow my eyes at the smile on his face, which only causes his smile to grow until his eyes light up with mirth.

"What?" I snap. Geez. What is wrong with me? I shouldn't be snapping at my boss.

Pops doesn't take offense. "The pub is opening in five minutes."

I look around the room. I'm nearly finished cleaning, but there are a few tables in the back I need to re-do as there were some funky stains, I don't want to think about, on them.

"I need another fifteen minutes."

"Take your time, Faith," he says and walks away.

My heart twinges at hearing him call me Faith. He's never called me Faith before. It's always been darling or spitfire. I guess my message about not wanting a relationship with him came across loud and clear. And no, I am not disappointed.

The door opens and I hear his Army buddies barge inside. *This is not the time to feel sorry for yourself, Faith. You have work to do.* I pick up my bucket and march to the troublesome tables.

It takes more than fifteen minutes to finish up and by the time I'm ready to call it a morning, the pub is hopping. Oh great. I look like I went ten rounds with Mike Tyson while everyone else in here is in business attire. I hug the edges of the room as I walk toward the hallway and freedom. I don't make it far.

"Hey, Faith. How's it going, doll?" Lenny greets as I try to rush past their table.

I force a smile upon my face. "I'm fine. How are you?" Fine. Ugh. I hate the word fine.

"Why are men like diapers?" Barney asks with a leer upon his face.

I grimace. Barney tells the worst jokes. They're either dirty or childish and nothing in between.

"They're usually full of shit but thankfully disposable."

Yep, dirty, but I can't help from remarking, "You're not wrong."

"What did one butt cheek say to the other?"

Oops. I guess I should have kept my mouth shut. I know better than to encourage a man.

"Together, we can stop this shit," he says and guffaws.

Pops marches over to the table. "I told you. No dirty jokes around Faith." I roll my eyes. I have a teenage son. I've heard more poop jokes than he can imagine.

"Ah, come on," Barney pleads. "We're all adults here. Faith has a kid. I think she knows how A slots into B."

Pops scowls. "Faith is a lady. There will be no crude talk in front of her." He glares down at his friends. "Do you understand?"

Wally smirks. "Yeah, brother, we get you." He winks at me before addressing the rest of the group, "I've got one month."

"What's he talking about?" I ask Pops. One month? "Are they betting?"

Pops nostrils flare. "They are not betting."

"Yeah, sure, Pops. Whatever you say," Barney says. I have a teenage kid, I can recognize a brush off when I hear one.

Apparently, Pops can too because he slams his hands down on the table and leans forward to declare, "Hear this, you will not bet about any relationship Faith and I have."

I gasp. They're betting about me and Pops? He stands and grasps my hands. "And, hear this, Spitfire, we will be having a relationship."

I yank my hands out of his grasp and place them on my hips. "And, hear this, Pops, we are not having a relationship."

Sid laughs. "Oh, this is going to be fun. I'm in. Who's got two months?"

I can't listen to this. They are all crazy. Before I can stomp away, Pops seizes my arm. "I told you, you don't call me Pops. To you, I'm Max."

"Did I say two months? Put me down for two weeks."

At Sid's words, a vein in Pops' forehead starts to pulse. He opens his mouth to respond to Sid, but I'm done.

"I don't have time for this. I need to get to work."

Pops freezes. "Get to work? You are at your work."

I roll my eyes. "My other job."

A muscle ticks in his jaw. "You're working two jobs and taking care of a kid on your own?"

What is his problem? "Um, yeah. And I'm late." I tilt my head toward where his hand is still holding my arm. He immediately lets go and steps back.

"We're talking about this later."

I wave a hand. Whatever. Time to make my escape. My escape is once again thwarted when I walk past a table of middle-aged businessmen and one of them pinches my ass.

I stop and twirl around to face them. "Did one of you pinch my ass?"

The noise in the room dies down at my question. Great. I don't need an audience for this, but I will not back down. It's up to me to teach my son how a man treats a woman. And, in order to do that, I need to show him how I, as a woman, expect to be treated by men. His father notwithstanding of course.

"I'll ask you one more time. Did one of you pinch my ass?"

I feel Pops take a step closer, but I hold up my hand to stop him. This is my problem to deal with. I won't hide behind a man. I cross my arms over my chest and commence a stare down. I have a teenage boy, I can do this all damn day.

The man closest to me crumples in seconds. "I'm sorry. It was me."

It's lesson time. "What makes you think it's okay to pinch the ass of a woman you don't know?"

His cheeks flush. "It's not?"

"You sound like you're asking me and not telling me. Let's try this again. Is it okay to touch a woman you don't know without permission?"

His face pales. "Without permission?" he squeaks.

"Yes, whether it's a pinch or a kiss or something more, you do not touch a woman unless she gives you her permission."

"Fuck." He buries his face in his hands. "I didn't think. I saw this gorgeous woman and I acted."

I snort. Gorgeous? Not likely. I'll admit my hair is pretty nice. The brown locks fall in waves down my back. But the rest of me is nothing to write home about. My eyes are entirely too dark. Brown, almost black, eyes are not the type men fantasize about. And my mouth is way too big. When I smile, it takes over my entire face, and not in a good way. And then there's my body. If it weren't for the wrinkles on my face and the occasional gray hair, I could be mistaken for a pre-pubescent girl with no hips or boobs to speak of.

Gorgeous woman or not, I need to make my point with this man. "But you won't be touching a woman without her permission again, will you?"

He lifts his head and faces me. "No, ma'am. I will not."

"Good."

"If you don't claim her Pops, I'll take her," Sid yells from across the room because apparently, this is *put Faith in the spotlight and embarrass her* day.

"Did you and Mary Ann break up again?" Wally asks.

"No. Never mind. I concede. The little firecracker is all yours."

Pops claims my hand. "Out," he orders the man. "You're banned."

The man's face falls, but he doesn't argue. He stands and drops a twenty on the table before sulking away. "I'm sorry," he says as he walks past.

"Show's over, folks," Pops shouts before dragging me across the pub and into the hallway where he pushes me against the wall and crowds me with his body flush against mine. Butterflies flap their wings in my stomach, but I tell them to knock that shit off. I don't have time for butterflies.

"You okay?"

The butterflies I barely beat into submission come out again. Why does he have to be sweet? I can't resist a sweet man. "I'm fine. It isn't the first time a man pinched my ass, and it won't be the last."

He growls. "It will be the last time it happens in my pub."

"Good. Now, let me go, I need to get to work."

He doesn't let me go. "We need to talk about you having two jobs."

We are never talking about me having two jobs. It's none of his damn business. I don't say anything of the sort, though. I know better than to offer a man like Pops a challenge. I'm not stupid after all. "Not now. I'm late."

He studies my face for a moment before taking a step back. "Go. We'll talk later."

Not if I can help it, we won't.

Chapter 3

When I tell my son, I'll do something in a minute, what I'm really saying is 'please for the love of all that's holy forget'.

I look at the clock. Darn it. A mere five minutes have passed since the last time I looked. Once the clock hits four, I have exactly thirty minutes to rush across town in time to catch Ollie's soccer game. I refuse to miss a game. It's bad enough my son will never have a dad at the sidelines since Silas washed his hands clean of us. I'm not going to let him down, too.

"Go." My co-worker Lisa shoves me toward the door. "I'll cover for you."

I open my mouth to tell her she doesn't need to, but she stops me with a pointed finger. "Stop. You've done the same for me when I needed to get out of here for one of Dane's hockey games."

I bite my lip. It's wrong to leave work early, isn't it?

"Go. Before I kick your butt out of here."

"Thank you," I whisper before I rush out of the room and out of the law firm.

Traffic across town slows me down, but I make it to the stadium five minutes before kickoff. I praise the goddess of single mothers when I notice a stand selling coffee. I treat myself to a cappuccino before finding a seat. Considering it's barely September, it's chilly with the wind whipping off the lake. I am not looking forward to winter in Wisconsin. Brrr. At least it's dry. Washing the mud out of Ollie's soccer gear in the ancient washing machine our rental apartment came with is not my idea of a fun Saturday afternoon.

"You new here?" the woman next to me asks.

I give her my 'tired mom but we're all in this together' look. "Yeah." I stick out my hand. "Faith."

"Rachel," she says as she shakes my hand. She points to the other women on the bench. "This is Tammy, Sharon, and Deb." They all wave in my direction.

"Which one's yours?"

"Ollie. Oliver." I point to where he's standing on the sidelines waiting for the game to begin.

"The one coach is excited about?" Tammy asks.

What? The coach is excited about Ollie's playing? When did this happen? And why don't I know about it? Crap. I haven't been paying enough attention to my kid. I suck. Single mom – Zero. Universe – One.

"No," Deb responds. "Not Oliver. The kid's name was Oscar."

Tammy shrugs. "I knew the name started with an O."

Phew. I'm not a completely horrible mom then. I erase the one from the universe's side of the scoreboard.

Rachel points to a kid jumping up and down on the sideline. "The kid who looks like he needs to pee is mine."

The other mothers point to their children, and I try to commit the names to memory, but I know from experience I won't remember them. There's a reason I call all of Ollie's friends honey after all. And it's not only because it embarrasses the hell out of my son.

We watch as the ref comes onto the field and the players take their positions for kickoff. "I hope my kid remembered to wear his white underwear today," Tammy mutters with her eyes pinned on her son as if she's superman with x-ray vision and can see right through his shorts to what underwear he chose to wear today.

Me, on the other hand, I don't have a care what color my kid's underwear is. I'm just happy when he remembers to put on a clean pair.

"He thought it would be funny to wear SpongeBob briefs under his white uniform shorts," she explains. "The girls were not amused, and the teasing commenced. After that, he made me buy him a truckload of tighty-whities."

"Nothing wrong with a pair of tighty-whities," Deb declares in a loud voice, and everyone on the bench in front of her swivels around to glare at her. "What? I'm not wrong."

Before we can get into a discussion of the benefits of tighty-whities versus other types of underwear, the ref blows the whistle, and the game begins. It takes approximately two point one seconds before I learn the women on my bench are not quiet observers.

"What are you doing?" Rachel screams when her kid slips on the ball and falls on his butt. Poor kid looks like his face went up in flames. "Get up!"

Her son forces himself to his feet and trails after the team as they run offense down the field. They pass the halfway line and break away from their opponents. As they run toward the penalty area, I notice the goal is empty. I jump to my feet with the rest of the crowd. A quick kick and they'll be in the lead. Except the kid with the ball fumbles.

"Awesome. Mr. Fumble is mine," Tammy mumbles before raising her voice. "Keep it together, Todd! You got this!"

Note to self: Bring ear plugs to soccer games from now on.

"Come on, come on," Sharon murmurs as she watches another player who I assume is her kid take control of the ball and move toward the goal. "Kick it in. Kick it in."

The kid hauls his right leg back, aims to shoot, and – bam! – he kicks. The ball misses the empty goal and hits a crossbeam before careening out of bounds. The crowd erupts in boos, and several people aim their glares toward Sharon.

I pat her shoulder. "He'll get it next time."

"Yeah, Shar," Deb adds. "At least he didn't moon the entire stadium this time."

What kind of team does Ollie's high school have? Are they the Bad News Bears of soccer?

My phone rings and shuts off thoughts of how the Bad News Bears managed to get out of their slump. Shoot. I forgot to switch it off when I arrived. I take it out of my bag and hurry to answer when I see who's calling.

"Faith?" Special Agent Judson asks.

"It's me. Hold on." I mouth *sorry* to the other mothers and then scramble down the stands until I'm behind the bleachers and away from the crowd where I can hear. "Sorry. I needed to find somewhere quiet. I'm at Ollie's soccer game."

"How's the kid doing?" he asks.

"Good," I answer, despite not being sure if I'm telling the truth. I like to think Ollie's good. He seems to be making friends and has joined tons of after school activities, but who can really tell when a surly teenager is involved?

"Can we go home?" I ask before Judson can say another word.

"I'm sorry, Faith, but no. It's not yet safe for Ollie or you for that matter."

I don't care about my safety, but I won't put Ollie in jeopardy despite the danger being of his own making. Stupid savior complex. I have no idea where it comes from. Not from his dad, that's for dang sure.

"But it's been a year." I hate the sound of my whining, but I am done with living in limbo. Done with working two menial jobs because I can't use my real name. Done with living a lie. Done. Done. Done.

Judson chuckles. "It's been nine months."

"Do you have children, Judson?"

"Two daughters."

"Are they teenagers?"

"My oldest is ten going on forty."

"Then you know. It hasn't been nine months. Hell, it hasn't been a year. It's been a freaking decade."

"I hear you." He pauses. "Is Ollie not settling in?"

"I guess. I don't know."

"Is he getting into fights? How are his grades?"

I sigh. I hear what he's saying loud and clear. "No, no fights. And his grades are as good as ever. The kid is a genius. How that happened is beyond me."

Judson's voice softens. "I'm sure it had something to do with his awesome mom."

I murmur some nonsensical reply, the same as any other time someone calls me an awesome mom. If they only knew. Most days I'm happy the kid is living when the sun sets. And there are those days I seriously can't manage to rouse a care for whether his underwear is clean or not.

"Listen, I need to go. You call if you need anything, and I'll let you know when it's safe to head home."

"Thanks for calling, Judson," I say and ring off.

As soon as I hear the beep to indicate the call is disconnected, I let my head fall forward and slump against the bleachers. Damn. When I saw Judson's name on my phone, hope flared. Stupid. I should know better. No getting my hopes up. They're destined to be dashed again and again.

I know the situation in Saint Louis is a mess. The FBI can't simply snap their fingers and resolve the disaster my son created. No, it's a delicate balancing act to keep the gangs from erupting in violence. Stupid gangs. And stupid me for not knowing there were gangs at Ollie's school.

Why, oh why, did Oliver have to stick his nose where it didn't belong? *Ugh. Stop feeling sorry for yourself, Faith. You would have kicked his ass if he had let those boys do what they were planning to do to that poor girl.*

I don't understand how I can be proud of my son and want to wring his neck at the same time. I guess that's motherhood for you.

Chapter 4

Dear Monday, My momma don't like you, and she likes everyone.

"Welcome to *You Cheat, We Eat*!" Hailey greets as I walk into the PI firm, she owns with Suzie, on Monday morning.

At least someone is excited to see me, Ollie couldn't get out of the car fast enough when I dropped him at school this morning. I hope we're not entering the 'I'm embarrassed of my mom'-portion of the teenage years. I will not handle those years well.

"Hi!" I wave like the dork I am. "Suzie asked me to fill in for her today. She said something about a big order and needing to bottle like her life depended on it."

"She told me. I'm glad you could come in. I'm worried we're going to have to hire a replacement for Suzie soon."

"At least we can lower our liability insurance then," Phoebe shouts from an office to the right of me. I peek in and wave to her. She stands and walks over, but her fiancé, Ryker, merely grunts in greeting. My lips purse of their own accord. A grunt is not a greeting. If he were my child, he would know better.

"Suzie isn't such a klutz anymore. Not since Grayson tamed her," Hailey says.

My eyes widen at the words 'tamed her'. "A man shouldn't tame a woman. He should love and cherish her. Taming shouldn't be involved."

Ryker grunts again from the other room. I'm not going to comment on the rudeness of grunting as a means of communication. Not everyone needs to hear a lecture from 'Bossy Mom' as my son likes to refer to me when he's not getting his way. Instead, I'm going to interpret his grunt to mean *I agree* and move on.

Phoebe and Hailey take seats in the reception area and look for all intents and purposes as if they're settling in for a chat. What's going on here? It's not like I'm friends with Pops' daughter and her friends. We're friendly since they're always hanging out at the pub, but that's it. There's no reason for a friendly catch-up.

"Is there a man in your life trying to tame you?" Hailey asks, and I nearly swallow my tongue in surprise at her boldness. She's crazy if she thinks I'm going to discuss my love life or lack thereof with her. I barely discuss it with my oldest and dearest friend Valerie, and she's not my boss's daughter.

"Um, no. No men for me." I look around the area for a distraction. The reception area contains a large desk with files piled high upon it. Several chairs are scattered throughout the area. The room is a study in wood paneling. It's not hideous, but it does remind me of those old-fashioned detective shows like *Ironside*.

"What do you need me to do?"

They ignore my question. "Then, you're currently not in a relationship?" Hailey asks instead.

I narrow my eyes on her. "I don't know how my relationship status is relevant to the work I need to do today." I tap my watch. "Tick tock."

"Are you open to a relationship?"

At Phoebe's question, I nearly explode. But I don't. Not when one day of pay from Hailey's PI firm is equivalent to three days of my filing job at the law firm. I take a deep breath and answer her question instead. "No."

Hailey jumps to her feet. "Good. I'm finally going to win a bet with my uncles."

"Your dad put a stop to any bets about whether or not your dad and I will pursue a relationship," I tell her.

She freezes. "Oh, she has the mom voice down pat."

I roll my eyes. Of course, I have the mom voice down pat, I am a mom.

Hailey grins. "Let me show you what we need you to do."

The rest of the morning passes quickly as I file client dossiers and answer the phone. I'm surprised how busy the place is. I knew Hailey and Phoebe were PIs in a business owned by Hailey and Suzie, but, despite Pops' bragging, I had no idea how successful the business is. Good for them.

I look up from the dwindling pile of dossiers when the bell over the door rings. I paste a smile on my face. "Welcome to *You Cheat, We Eat*. How may I help you?"

"I need to hire a private investigator," the woman says.

"Please. Have a seat. Can I get you something to drink?"

She sits but shakes her head to decline a beverage. "When can you begin?"

Someone's in a hurry. I open a drawer and remove an intake sheet. "Why don't you tell me your name and why you need a PI?"

"My name is Tanya Whittaker. I need an investigator to follow the investigator I already hired."

This is a bit bizarre, but nothing I can't handle. "Can you explain why you need your PI followed?"

Behind me, I hear Hailey stand and walk to the door. Thank goodness. I have no idea what I'm doing. My question is the result of curiosity, not anything resembling a clue as to what I'm doing.

Tanya huffs. "Duh, to make sure he does his job."

"Um, if you don't trust your investigator, why don't you fire him and hire a new one?"

She rolls her eyes. "Because I hired him to do a job. I paid him to do a job. And he will do his job."

Hailey approaches and offers Tanya her hand. "Tanya, was it? I'm Hailey Barnes. Why don't you step into my office and we can talk further?"

I exhale in relief when Tanya follows Hailey. I didn't think about what little knowledge I have of the PI business when I agreed to help out for the day. I sit at the desk and organize files while Hailey deals with her. They walk out of the office not five minutes later. Hailey shakes her hand and escorts her out the door.

"What happened?" I ask once the Tanya's gone.

Hailey wrinkles her brow at me for a second before she snorts a laugh. "Oh yeah, I forgot. You're not Suzie." I must look confused because she explains. "Suzie always eavesdrops at the door."

"Like I am right now." Phoebe walks out from behind the door to her office.

I guess they don't value their privacy. Silly women. I would kill for privacy in my life. "Why do you bother with separate offices?"

Hailey grins. "Because my husband likes to visit." She wiggles her eyebrows at me.

My face heats, and I raise my hands to ward off any further revelations. "Too much information."

Ryker walks into the room. "I'm going for lunch. Who wants to place an order?"

I lift my bag up. "I brought a sandwich." I don't bother adding I don't want to spend money on lunch. They don't need to hear about my penny-pinching ways.

Hailey wrinkles her nose. "You're not eating a sandwich from home. I'll have my usual times two." When I go to protest, she stops me. "My treat. I owe you for agreeing to come in last minute after all."

Ryker marches out of the room. He doesn't look like a happy camper.

"What's wrong with him?"

Phoebe collapses in a chair. "He's mad at me."

"What did you do now?" Hailey looks at me and explains. "Phoebe is dragging her feet about the wedding."

"Are you getting cold feet?" I ask. "It's perfectly normal to be nervous."

Phoebe shakes her head. "Nah, I want to marry the big lug."

I immediately move into problem-solving mode. "Then, what's the problem and how can I help?"

"There are too many decisions to make. Suzie said if I hired a wedding planner, I wouldn't have to make all these decisions, but the wedding planner sends me messages with all kinds of questions constantly!"

I wait to make sure Phoebe is done complaining before asking, "What kind of questions?"

"What kind of flowers do I want? What are my colors? What do the bridesmaids' dresses look like? Have I picked a band from the demo tapes she provided? What kind of cake do I want? Do I approve of the seating plan? It goes on and on and on."

None of those questions sound too difficult.

My confusion must show on my face because Hailey explains, "Phoebe was married before. She thinks if she makes one wrong decision it's going to ruin this marriage."

I slap a hand over my mouth before my giggle can escape. Like a wedding – good or bad – has a single thing to do with the success of a marriage.

"It's okay. You can laugh at her. We do all the time."

I am not going to laugh at her. I frown at Hailey. "It's not nice to laugh at someone who is genuinely struggling. You should know better." I wait until she looks contrite before addressing Phoebe, "As for you, what is your favorite flower?"

"Tulip."

"Then your wedding flowers will be tulips."

"But they're expensive this time of year."

I indicate her outfit with my hand. I'm not into fashion, but I'm not an idiot. I know those pumps with red soles are more expensive than my car.

Phoebe flexes her foot. "These are from my previous life."

Hailey scoffs. "It's not like you're destitute now. Someone is Ms. Moneybags."

"What's the problem, then?"

Phoebe bites her lip. "I don't want to shove my money into everyone's faces. It's what my family does."

"Makes sense." I take a moment to think before announcing, "Tulips are not usually expensive flowers. Most of the guests won't realize they're out of season and therefore more expensive right now. Next question."

Phoebe's mouth drops open as she stares at me. I wiggle my fingers at her in a 'bring it on' motion. She clears her throat. "My colors."

By the time Ryker returns with our lunch, we've gone through several emails of questions from the wedding planner and resolved every single one of them. Easy peasy.

"You're like a wedding savant. Are you a wedding planner in disguise?" Phoebe asks as she puts her phone away and takes a burger from Ryker.

I snort. "No. I'm a single mother of a teenager. There's no time to second guess decisions and time planning is essential."

Hailey nods. "I get it. My dad was a single parent. Single parents are like superheroes without the cool outfits."

"I wish my son agreed with you," I mutter and then take a huge bite of my burger before I can continue to run my mouth and reveal all my insecurities to them.

Hailey pats my hand. "Trust me. He might not appreciate it now, but he will someday," she says as if it's a foregone conclusion.

I hope she's right.

Chapter 5

And then I thought to myself, what's the point of cleaning if my son is going to keep living here?

I LOOK UP WHEN I hear the door open the next day at McGraw's Pub. I check the clock to see if I'm running late. No, I'm right on time and have another hour to finish cleaning before the pub opens for lunch. Wally is early is all.

He strolls toward me and clears his throat before asking, "Can we talk?"

My nose wrinkles of its own accord. He sounds serious. "Is there a problem?"

"Not exactly."

I know man-speak. After all, I have a mini-man at home. *Not exactly* means *Yes, we have a problem and it's going to ruin your day*. Crap. What now?

Wally frowns at me. "Don't freak out."

Does he know nothing about women? We do the exact opposite of what a man tells us to do. It's like a built-in biological mechanism. There's nothing I can do about it. I have to freak out now. My hands shake as I lean the mop against the bar.

"Shall we sit down?" he asks before leading me to a chair.

Sit down? It's worse than I thought! What did I do wrong? Oh no, have those thugs from Saint Louis found us? Damn it. We're going to have to move again. I was actually beginning to like Milwaukee. A little voice in my head says there's a certain someone in Milwaukee I am especially liking, but I ignore the voice. It's the same voice that told me to marry Silas after all.

"Calm down."

I've had enough now. "Calm down! How do you expect me to calm down? You waltz in here saying we need to talk and then say there's a problem and we have to sit down. Sit down!"

"Whoa! Slow down!" He holds up his hands. "I never said there was a problem."

I point at him. "Yes, you did. You said 'not exactly' when I asked if there's a problem. If that's not an admission of there being a problem, I don't know what is."

He runs a hand over the closely cropped hair on his head. "Damn, woman. You are too smart for your own good."

Smart? If I were smart, I wouldn't be mopping the floors of a pub. But I'm not going to debate my intelligence with him. No, I need to know what the hell is going on right now. "What's wrong? What's the problem? And how can we fix it?"

He smiles. "A problem solver. I like it."

I throw my hands in the air. "Can you stop with the analysis of my character and intelligence and tell me what the hell is going on here?"

The smile drops from his face. "I did a background check on you."

My heart rate speeds up and sweat forms on my brow. He can't know who I am. It's dangerous for Ollie. And I have to keep Ollie safe. I have to! "You did what?" I screech.

"It's customary to do a background check on employees."

I narrow my eyes at him. "There's one problem with your statement." I lean in close and snarl at him. "I'm not your employee."

He doesn't respond to my comment. He goes in for the kill instead. "I came up against a stonewall when I ran your name. What's going on, kid?"

Kid? Is he seriously calling me a kid? I'm a forty-five-year-old single mother. Kid is the last word I'd use to describe me. My nose flares. "I'm not a kid." But I may be using juvenile tactics to force this conversation away from where it's heading.

Wally waves away my complaint. "Sorry."

I ignore Wally's lame-ass apology. I don't have time to delve deeper into who he thinks he is doing a background check on me. I need to call Agent Judson and make sure no one has found out our location. I stand. I need to get out of here. If a certain group has discovered our location, I don't have much time to pack. Good thing the furniture in our rental apartment is thrift store finds I don't mind abandoning.

"Sit down. We're not done talking."

I ball my hands into fists. He did not just order me around, did he? No one – and I do mean no one – orders me around anymore. I hiss at him. "I don't follow orders from you."

"If you don't tell me why I ran into a stonewall when I did a background check on you, we're going to have bigger problems than you being mad at me."

"I don't have to tell you a single thing." And I don't. He's not the boss of me.

"I will not allow someone to be around my friends and family who is hiding secrets."

I snort. Oh, he won't allow it, will he?

"I'm serious. I'm not afraid to tell Pops what I learned."

"Tell Pops what?"

I yelp and jump when I hear Pops' voice right behind me. He places a hand on my hip to settle me and my traitorous body breaks out in goosebumps. He's not even touching my skin and there are goosebumps. Do I need a bigger 'danger ahead' sign? No, I do not. I take a step away. He frowns but lets his hand drop.

Wally stands and crosses his arms over his chest. "I did a background check on Faith."

"You did what? How dare you?" Pops bellows before looking at me. "I'm sorry, Faith. I didn't tell him to do a background check."

"After all the troubles we've had in the past year, I couldn't risk you falling in love with someone who is hiding a secret."

Falling in love? I wheeze and struggle for a breath. He can't mean me? We barely know each other. Except we've spent more time having coffee together these past months than the time I spent over the years with Silas, and I was married to the ass. Things are getting complicated.

Pops rubs circles in my back. "Breathe, sweetheart. Just breathe. No one's going to dig into your background."

Wally growls. "Yes, we are. She could be dangerous. Or have dangerous people after her. We need to be prepared."

Pops' hand drops from me, and he takes a step toward Wally. "Didn't you learn your lesson the first time you pried into Faith's life? The dyed blue hair wasn't enough of a clue for you?"

Is that why Wally had blue hair? Despite everyone bugging the hell out of him, he wouldn't admit what prompted the prank from Pops. I can't help the snort from escaping. Seeing Wally, aka the most uptight man in the world, with blue hair was hilarious.

And I'm not kidding about the whole most uptight thing. The man defines the word. He wears his black hair in a high and tight haircut despite being retired from the military for years now. His jeans and button-down shirts are always ironed without a speck of dirt on them. And his dark green eyes constantly survey any room he's in as if he's looking for trouble. Like I said, uptight.

"I don't give a crap what you do to me. But her," Wally points at me, "she's dangerous and you know it."

"I'm not dangerous. I'm a single mom of a teenage boy working two jobs to make ends meet. Pathetic comes to mind, not dangerous."

Pops moves to stand in front of me and places his hands on my shoulders. "You are not pathetic. You are a warrior doing what you need to do to ensure your kid has everything he needs and wants. And it's sexy as all get out."

I try to move away, but he squeezes my shoulders. "Do you get me yet? Am I getting through?" I take a step back. "No, I'm not getting through. I will. I'm not giving up."

"Neither am I," Wally announces. "I will dig and dig until I figure out what you're hiding."

This is not good. I know Agent Judson gave us new last names and did some mumbo jumbo with our backgrounds to make us disappear, but I'm afraid someone with Wally's skills can find out more. Suzie and Hailey don't call him the super-secret agent for nothing. But if he goes digging around, he's going to alert other people of where we are living. I can't have that.

"Will you stop digging if I quit?" My voice trembles, but I clear my throat and straighten my spine. I can do this. I can quit and find another cleaning job. "And I promise not to come around again?"

Wally shakes his head. "Kid, I don't want you to quit. I want to know who you are."

"You're not quitting and that's final," Pops declares.

I rise up on my toes to get up in his face. "You can't order me around." I take a step back. "And I do quit."

My heart squeezes and tears well in my eyes. I thought Wally was a friend. But friends don't act like he did. I blink my eyes to stop the tears from falling. I will not show Wally how much he's hurt me. I am done with letting men hurt me.

Pops reaches for me. "Faith, my spitfire."

I take another step back and his hand falls. When he steps forward, I hold up my hand. "No. I quit, and we're done." We didn't get much of a chance to get started, but it's better this way. This way no one gets hurt. My heart squeezes. Too much. No one gets hurt too much.

"Have a nice life." I wave, because even when my heart is breaking, I'm a dork, and walk away. I don't bother picking up my cleaning supplies. If I take the time to be neat, I'm going to lose the thin hold I have on my emotions.

I walk straight out the front door but have to lean against the wall of the building when my legs threaten to collapse from beneath me. I can't believe I walked away. It's for the better. I can't have Ollie in danger.

I hear a crash behind me and then shouting. I need to get the hell out of here before I hear things I don't want to hear. I straighten my shoulders and walk to my car.

I'm okay. I'm okay. I'm okay.

Chapter 6

Have you ever looked at those piles and piles of laundry and considered just throwing all the clothes away?

"I don't care if Andy is your best friend forever and is having a birthday today. It's a school night, and you'll finish your homework. Then, if there's time, you may go to his house for one hour and one hour only."

Ollie glares at me, but I'm not backing down. Back down once and he'll think I'll back down the next time and pretty soon I'm a pushover. Ollie's eyes drop, and he stomps off to get his schoolbooks. Yes! Single Mom – One. Universe – Zero. Although, I may need to reevaluate my point system now that my kid has entered his whiny teenage years.

I return to the kitchen and preparing dinner as Ollie slams his books onto the kitchen table. The doorbell rings, and he yells, "I'll get it."

Not on my watch, he won't. I point to his books. "Homework."

He scowls as he collapses in his chair, and I walk to the door. I'm totally racking up single mom points today. Take that,

Universe! I grunt when I look through the peephole and see who's standing there. I knew he wouldn't let this go.

"Open the door, Faith. I know you're in there," Pops says.

"You don't have X-ray vision. You can't see through the door," I say because I'm a dorky idiot.

He chuckles. "No, but I can see your shadow."

I also opened my big fat mouth and let him know I was home. I open the door but keep my hand on it using my arm to block him from entering. He raises an eyebrow at my arm but doesn't comment. "What do you want?"

"Yeah, what are you doing here?" I look to the heavens and pray for some patience with my son.

"Homework," I remind him. His response? He crosses his arms over his chest and glares at Pops. My teenage boy thinks he's protecting me. He even went to McGraw's Pub to bitch Pops out when he thought my boss was hitting on me. Pops backed off after their encounter, until he threw down the gauntlet at Suzie's wedding party.

"Can I talk to your mom alone, son?"

Ollie snarls. "I am not your son, and you may not talk to my mom alone. You fired her and hurt her feelings."

He had to mention hurting my feelings, didn't he? Although it would be hard for him to miss me being all emotional today. In addition to quitting my job, I had to call Agent Judson and warn him someone is looking into my background. He was not amused.

"He didn't fire me. I quit."

"You quit because he was being an asshole. It's the same as being fired."

"Language!" I admonish, although my heart is nearly bursting with pride for him sticking up for his old ma.

"Sorry, Ma." Ollie doesn't look sorry at all. He's glaring at Pops for all he's worth. To Pops' credit, he's not laughing at my son. He's looking at him with respect, and there go the butterflies in my stomach again.

"Can I come in? I'd prefer not to have a serious discussion while standing in the hallway in view of your neighbors."

Neighbors. Shoot. I forgot all about my neighbors. Mrs. Lebowski down the hall is the biggest snoop in existence. I stick my head into the hallway and sure enough, she's standing in front of her door not bothering to disguise her eavesdropping. Great. Just great. Everyone in the apartment building will know I had a gentleman caller before the morning.

I motion Pops into the apartment. He doesn't move. He waits for me to go inside first. I roll my eyes and walk to the tiny living room where we take seats on opposite ends of the sofa. Ollie perches himself on the armrest next to me.

"Nice place you got here," Pops says as he looks around.

"Do not patronize me." This place is not nice. Clean? Yes. Nice? Not on your life. It's half the size of our apartment in Saint Louis. Ollie's bedroom is not much bigger than a closet. In fact, I think it may have been a closet at one time considering how little storage this place has.

I motion for him to get on with it. "What do you want? Ollie needs to finish his homework. He has a birthday party to attend."

"It's fine, Ma. I don't need to go to the birthday party."

No way! This is not happening. "You are not giving up a party you've been arguing to attend for the past half-hour because Pops showed up uninvited."

"I'll make this quick then," Pops says before Ollie can respond. I nod for him to continue. "I want you to come back to work."

"No." I shake my head. "I will not have one of your friends digging around in my life."

Ollie gulps. "You quit because someone was digging around in our past?"

I pat his arm. "It's not your fault." He may have been the catalyst for what happened, but I will not blame my son for being a hero. Not today, at least.

Pops looks from me to my son, and his eyes see entirely too much. I need to hurry this along before he figures out why our past needs to stay buried in our past. I stand. "If there's nothing else."

"I'm not finished. I want you to come back to work, and I promise Wally won't dig into your past anymore."

"You can't make a promise on behalf of someone else."

"I sure as hell can, and I am."

"Ma." Ollie tugs on my sleeve until I sit back down on the sofa. "Maybe you should consider his offer."

"You know why I can't accept his offer," I say in a soft voice. He's been hurt enough with the situation, I don't need to make it worse by being curt with him.

"Speaking of offers, I'll double your salary," Pops announces.

My eyes widen. "Are you out of your mind? No one pays cleaners double minimum wage."

"And I'll give you benefits."

"What kind of benefits?" Ollie asks.

I need to shut this shit down. "You are not going to double my salary and give me benefits because you want to get in my pants."

Ollie growls. Fan-freaking-tastic. Did I seriously say those words in front of my son? Single Mom – Minus Fifty. Universe – One Gazillion. Good thing I wipe the slate clean each morning. I would never be getting out of the hole I dug otherwise.

Pops snarls. "I'm not offering to increase your salary because I want you. You've been working for me for nine months. I should have increased your salary at six months. And a benefits package is available once you've worked for me for one year. I'm moving up the timeline is all."

Ollie bumps me with his shoulder. "You need to accept this. You can quit the job at the law office. You're always bitching about how boring it is there and how you would do things better. And you won't be exhausted all the time from working two jobs."

"Language," I say automatically before squeezing his hand. "You don't need to feel guilty for me working two jobs." He squirms but doesn't respond.

Silence falls on us until Pops grunts. "Listen to the kid. He's right and you know it."

I look between Ollie and Pops. "Don't tell me the men are ganging up on the women now."

Ollie shrugs, and Pops smirks. How can anyone be expected to fight against these two?

"Fine," I give in. A smile breaks out on Pops' face but when I continue it disappears. "But you will ensure Wally does not dig into my past. I'm serious. This is non-negotiable."

Pops extends his hand. "You have my word."

I look him in the eye to let him see exactly how serious I am before I shake his hand. He doesn't look victorious or smug. He looks into my eyes like he knows exactly what I'm hiding. I yank away my hand. I'm being fanciful. He can't read my mind.

Pops stands. "Now, who wants pizza for dinner?"

"I'm already making spaghetti."

"With meatballs," Ollie adds. I raise an eyebrow at him. Didn't he hate Pops like five minutes ago? Why is he encouraging him now? What is he up to?

"Spaghetti and meatballs, my favorite," Pops says in a blatant attempt to wrangle an invite for dinner.

Fortunately – or unfortunately, I'm not sure at this point – I didn't make enough to feed the three of us. "Sorry, but I only prepared enough for Ollie and me."

Pops stares at me for a long moment. I lock my limbs to stop myself from fidgeting. I wouldn't put it past him to march into the kitchen and look into the pot to check if I'm lying. Finally, he nods. "Okay, Spitfire. I'll give you this play."

I'm not playing. And this isn't some game.

"Why do you call Ma Spitfire?" Ollie asks.

Pops grins. "Have you met your ma? She's a spitfire."

Ollie laughs. "Yeah, you're right."

"Walk me out," Pops orders as he stands. I roll my eyes. The door is right there. It's literally three steps from the sofa.

"I need to finish my homework," Ollie announces in a loud voice. What does he think is happening here? And do I want to know?

Pops nabs my hand and drags me to the door. "I'll see you tomorrow, Spitfire?"

Ugh! Why does my tummy warm and butterflies appear every time he says the word spitfire? It's not like the word is a term of endearment. But with the way his voice lowers and deepens, he sure makes it sound like an endearment.

"Yeah," I manage to utter.

He bends forward and kisses my forehead. "Stay safe."

He leaves and the testosterone in the air lowers to the level of teenage hormonal boy. I push out a breath of relief. The man is entirely too dangerous. Whenever he touches me, I become a woman with desires and needs and forget all about being a single woman trying to keep her son out of danger. I'm not sure how long I can resist him. But resist him, I must.

I square my shoulders and march to the kitchen. There's no time to sit around and get all mushy over a man. I have food to make and birthday parties to attend.

Chapter 7

It's like my son doesn't realize let alone appreciate how I stayed up all night overthinking for him.

I'M NERVOUS WHEN I arrive to clean at McGraw's Pub the next morning, but when I unlock the door and enter, it's like every other morning – empty. Phew. I take a deep breath. I can do this. Five hours later, I'm nearly finished cleaning when Pops approaches me. It's the first time I've seen him today as we didn't do our morning coffee ritual. And no, I'm not upset about it. Not at all.

"Faith." He grins and my belly warms. I'm beginning to think I need a stomach transplant. The stupid organ does not listen to my head. "Can you stay for lunch today?"

My belly heats further, and the butterflies in my stomach take flight. "Um… I have to be at my other job by one."

He frowns and takes a step closer. "I thought you were quitting your second job."

Insert eye roll here. "I am, but I can't quit without notice." I don't mention that I tried to do the exact same thing to him. And lucky for his genitals, he doesn't mention it either.

He switches tactics. "If we eat at noon, will you have enough time to get to your second job?"

"Yeah," I add and try not to think what the effect of spending money on lunch will be on my groceries this week.

His nostrils flare. "You are not paying for lunch. All employees eat for free when they work during a mealtime."

I'm technically not working through lunch, but I choose to drop the subject. "All right. I need to finish up now though."

He nods and moves away to allow me to finish mopping the floor. Once the floor is spick and span, I stow away the cleaning supplies and then visit the restroom to freshen up my appearance. Lucky for me, I always bring a change of clothes as I can hardly show up at the law firm in the dusty clothes I've been sweating in all morning.

When I return to the pub, I notice Hailey, Suzie, and Phoebe are here.

"What's going on? Why is everyone here during lunch on a Thursday?" I ask.

"Wally pissed Pops off. We're waiting to see how Pops takes his revenge," Hailey explains.

Suzie bounces on her toes. "It's going to be epic," she sings.

Shit. Shit. Shit. Is this about me? Does everyone know what happened? "What happened? How did Wally piss him off?"

Hailey shrugs. "I don't know. No one's talking."

Thank goodness. No one knows about Wally's attempt to pry into my life.

Suzie snorts. "As if keeping secrets is unusual. Super-secret spy Wally never talks."

"I'm here for the food," Phoebe adds.

Hailey leans over and whispers, "Can you believe when we met her, she wouldn't eat anything remotely unhealthy? And now she's addicted to burgers and wings."

"Although she's still stuck up about her choice of beverage." Suzie purses her lips in disapproval. I guess she doesn't like Phoebe not enjoying the beers from her microbrewery.

Phoebe rolls her eyes. "Drinking vodka martinis is not stuck up." We all stare at her until she huffs. "Fine. Maybe it's a little stuck up."

Pops appears behind me. "Find a table, Babycakes," he tells Hailey. "I'll bring your food over in a minute."

I'm confused. "But I didn't order yet."

"As if I don't know what you like. A tuna melt and fries coming right up." He winks at me before taking off.

Hailey fans herself. "Is it hot in here? Maybe I should have picked an earlier date."

"Ixnay on the betting talk. Pops will have a fit," Suzie orders but grins like she's looking forward to Pops losing his mind.

I'm disappointed as I join the girls in a booth. I thought Pops wanted to have lunch with me. Am I misreading all the signals he's throwing out? And why do I care? I don't have time for a relationship I remind myself.

"The boys are back in the bar. The boys are back in the bar," Suzie sings as Lenny, Barney, Wally, and Sid walk in.

I look away. I have no desire to see or talk to Wally.

"You do realize those are not the lyrics to the song? And you're adding an extra syllable," Phoebe points out.

"I don't care," Suzie sings in response.

I search my mind for a topic other than the men the three of them refer to as their uncles. "How did the bottling go last week?" I ask Suzie.

"It went awesome!" She sticks her hands in the air as if celebrating a victory.

"How many bottles did you drop?" Hailey asks.

"Only four," she declares like dropping four bottles is a win.

"How's married life treating you?" Hailey wiggles her eyebrows.

Before Suzie has a chance to answer, there's a tap on my shoulder. I look up to see Wally standing there. Oh great.

"Can I have a moment of your time, please?"

It's the please that does it. I would be a bitch if I denied his request after he asked politely. I take a deep breath and stand. I follow as he leads me toward the back hallway. Pops watches the entire time with his eyes narrowed. When I raise my eyebrow at him, he tilts his head toward the hallway where Wally's waiting. We walk to the office where we can have some privacy.

"You know the girls are going to start a ton of rumors about this," I say before he has a chance to speak.

"Don't worry. Pops is distracting them." Do I want to know how he's distracting them? No, I decide. I do not.

"What do you want to talk about?" *Please don't say my past. Please don't say my past.* I've already given notice at my other job. They were none too pleased. I doubt they'd hire me back.

He runs a hand over his head. "I need to apologize."

My mouth falls open. I never expected those words to come out of his mouth.

"I was an ass."

If he's waiting for me to contradict him, he's going to be waiting a long damn time. He was an ass.

"Can I explain why?"

As I demonstrated earlier, I am not a bitch. Of course, he can explain. In fact, I want to know why he went completely alpha man crazy over a background check. I motion at him to get on with it.

"Do you know what happened to Phoebe?"

I shake my head. I've heard talk of kidnappings and such, but I don't know the whole story. I'm curious, but I didn't pry because it's none of my business. And there's the whole bit about me keeping secrets and not planning to reveal any of them in exchange for learning Phoebe's.

"She was using a false name," he starts. By the time he finishes, my jaw is hanging open. She was kidnapped not once but twice. I can't imagine the gorgeous, totally put together woman being kidnapped at all. And Ryker's part in the story? Who would have known?

"Now, do you understand why I lost it when I couldn't find out any information about you?" When I don't speak, he explains, "I was worried someone's after you."

"I promise I'm not putting anyone in danger by working here," I say because he deserves to hear the words. He doesn't need to hear how Ollie and I might be in danger. I'll make sure the danger never comes near them. I would never put Pops in jeopardy.

"Thank you. And, again, I apologize."

"I forgive you."

"Now, get out of here and have your lunch with the girls. I know you need to get to your second job."

I twirl around and leave the office to discover the girls are waiting for me. They motion me to the end of the hallway.

"What's going on?"

"Shhh…" Suzie orders in a voice way louder than mine when I asked my question.

Hailey pulls me to the side. "Watch," she says and points to Wally walking toward the restroom.

Wally enters the restroom but before the door can close, he's screaming like a little girl. I step forward to help him, but Hailey holds me back. "Wait."

The screaming ends, and the cursing begins. Wow. I've never even heard of half of the words he's muttering.

"Someone is a swearmeister," Phoebe says with wide eyes.

"Was he a sailor?" I ask.

Lenny growls from behind me. "We're former soldiers, not lame-ass seamen."

Alrighty then. If I want to offend anyone in the group, I now know how.

Wally comes barreling out of the restroom and marches down the hallway. We plaster ourselves to the wall to let him pass. "I'm going to kill your dad, Hailey."

Hailey shrugs as if she doesn't care. Considering how these guys are constantly pranking each other, she's probably heard the threat a lot in her lifetime.

"Come on." She tags my hand and leads me down the hallway to the men's restroom.

I'm not eager to walk into a room that made a scary man like Wally scream like a baby, but Hailey doesn't have such qualms. She pushes into the room, dragging me behind her.

My eyes widen when I see the clown at the urinal. It's not an actual clown. It's a pop-up of a clown. There are also balloons on the ceiling. I'm confused. Is this what scared Wally?

Hailey barks out a laugh. She's nearly hyperventilating and has to bend over to catch her breath. Suzie pushes her way in behind me and joins her laughter.

"It is kind of funny," Phoebe remarks as she comes to stand next to me. "The man has seen action in warzones, but a clown at a urinal has him nearly peeing his pants in fright."

When you put it like that… My lips tip up and the first giggle erupts.

As the four of us stand in the men's restroom giggling like teenagers, I can't help but let hope build that the current cycle of hell my life is on is coming to an end and an upswing is on its way. Fingers crossed.

Chapter 8

I Googled my symptoms. Turns out I just have a kid.

I slam my car door and run toward McGraw's Pub. Hailey called me thirty minutes ago in a complete panic about an emergency – a pipe burst, and the entire place is flooded. I need to get the place clean and dry before the pub opens up for the evening. I'm not sure how I'll manage, but I'm going to try. Thank goodness, Ollie is old enough to be left at home on his own.

I fling the door open and dash inside. I come to a screeching halt when I see the place. There's no burst pipe. There's no flood. Instead, some magical fairy has transformed the pub into a romantic setting with candles, flowers, and fairy lights. There are even rose petals on the ground leading to a table obviously set up for a romantic dinner.

I can smell garlic bread and cheese. My stomach rumbles in response.

Pops rushes in from the hallway. He sees me and sighs in relief. "You're all right. I thought…" His words trail off when he sees the look on my face. "What's wrong?"

"What's wrong?" I indicate the room with a sweep of my hand. "Your daughter is playing matchmaker is what's wrong."

He chuckles. "I should have known she was up to no good when I saw her carrying around a *Matchmaking for Dummies* book."

"There's a *Matchmaking for Dummies* book?" I shake my head. Who cares about a book right now? "What are we going to do?"

Pops takes my elbow and guides me to the table. "I think we should enjoy our lunch. It smells delicious."

My stomach rumbles again, but I drag my feet. "Don't you care your daughter set you up?"

He twirls me around to face him. "Why would I care when her scheming ends with me having lunch with the woman I want?"

I roll my eyes. "I told you. I'm not dating my boss."

"And I told you I'm done waiting."

I yank my arm away from him. Who does he think he is? Telling me he's done waiting. I have a say in whether I'm in a relationship or not. What am I thinking? This wouldn't be a relationship. Not when the man is still in love with his ex-wife.

"I'm not available for a roll in the hay."

His nostrils flare, and a vein in his forehead pulses. "Give me some credit. I want more from you and you know it."

"Know it?" I scoff. "You're in love with your ex-wife!"

Every muscle in his body tenses as he freezes. It feels as if all the air in the room has been sucked away. "You think I'm in love with my ex-wife?" he asks between clenched teeth.

Considering the anger coming in waves off of him, I suppress the urge to act like a child and tell him *duh*. "Everyone thinks it. You haven't dated since she left you."

"Come on." He takes my hand and leads me to the table. "I need a glass of wine for this conversation."

"You drink wine?" I slap my hand over my mouth. When will I stop saying stupid things and showing off my dorkiness?

Pops chuckles. "Yeah, I drink wine."

He pulls a chair out for me, and I take a seat at the over-the-top romantic table, which I secretly love. Candles, flowers, chocolates. I'll never admit it out loud, but I'm one of those girly girls who loves all the trappings of romance. Too bad I have absolutely zero experience with it. Silas wouldn't know what romance was if it hit him over the head. Hell, hitting him over the head didn't work either. Trust me. I tried.

Pops pours us each a glass of wine. I sip on mine. Noon on Sunday isn't a great time to guzzle wine. Pops apparently disagrees. He downs half the glass before speaking.

"I'm not in love with Lucy, my ex-wife. In fact, I don't think I ever was."

I can't help it. I snort. "Yeah, right."

He raises his brows and glares at me. "Are you going to let me tell the story?"

"Sorry." I take another sip of wine to keep my dorky mouth from opening again.

"My wife didn't leave me. I kicked her out." I slap a hand over my mouth to stop my gasp from escaping. I also lean closer. This I gotta hear.

"She was a crap mom. She wasn't like you whatsoever. You'd do anything for your kid – including work two menial jobs when you're obviously qualified for much more." He pauses, but I'm not falling into his trap. I am not telling him about my past and how we ended up here.

"Anyway, Lucy pretty much ignored Hailey. While I worked my ass off getting the pub up and running, Lucy was off shopping or hanging with her friends. She never got involved in Hailey's life. It was me taking her to ballet class and play practice. The worst was Hailey's birthday. She never bought her a cake or present. Frankly, I think she forgot what day her daughter was born on."

"Why did you put up with her?" I can't help myself from asking. How can a mother forget her own daughter's birthday? I would be mortified.

"Guilt. I knew she didn't want children, but when I got her pregnant on accident, I begged her to keep the baby. She didn't want her, but I thought once Hailey was here, she'd change her tune. I was wrong."

"And so, you kicked her out?"

He scratches his beard. "I put up with her for twelve long years before I confronted her and gave her a choice. Be a real mom to Hailey or leave. I didn't think she'd leave."

"Does Hailey know the truth?"

"Yeah." He frowns. "I had to tell her when she was dating Aiden. She was obviously not giving him a chance, assuming he'd leave her like her mom did."

"I bet that conversation went over well."

He grins. "My girl has a set of lungs on her. But once the screaming was done and she calmed down, she was actually relieved to know her mom hadn't abandoned her. She was mad I didn't tell her earlier, though. I would have, but I didn't realize she was suffering from 'textbook abandonment issues' as she called them."

I sit back in my chair. He's not in love with his wife? I look him up and down. Why in the world is he still single if he's not holding onto her memory?

He reaches across the table and takes my hand. "And now you know there's nothing standing in the way of us being together."

I'm not ready to leave the whole ex-wife situation. "If you're not in love with your ex, why haven't you been in a relationship before this?"

He wiggles his eyebrows. "I was waiting for the right woman to come along." I roll my eyes. Talk about cheesy. "I'm not yanking your chain. I've dabbled in dating, but I'm not going to settle for anyone less than the one. Been there. Done that."

And he thinks I'm the one? Gulp. Nope. I can't deal with that right now. "We can't date. You're my boss and you're too old for me."

He squeezes my hand. "Bullshit excuses."

"My reasons aren't bullshit."

"Sweetheart, they are, and you know it."

I narrow my eyes and glare at him. "Women don't like to be told they're full of bullshit."

He laughs. "There's my spitfire."

I'm beginning to think he gets off on fighting with me.

"Hell, yeah, I get off on fighting with you. It shows me you have passion. And I want all your passion directed at me."

Oh boy. Is it warm in here? I feel my cheeks heat along with other lower parts of my body.

He smirks like he knows the effect he's having on me. Who am I kidding? I'm probably oozing a gazillion pheromones now.

"Let's deal with your bullshit reasons one by one. Bullshit reason number one. I may own this place, but you come and go as you please. Hell, unless I make time to have coffee with you, I don't see you when you're working."

"But what about when it ends?"

His nostrils flare. "We are going to see where this goes. Hell, I'm half in love with you already."

The butterflies in my stomach flap their wings and then proceed to do cartwheels across my stomach. In love with me? "W-w-what?"

He ignores my question. "As for age, what the hell, Spitfire? I'm fifty-six and you're forty-five. Eleven measly years. We're both adults. Both single parents."

I have no response. Bringing up his age was me grasping at straws. Lord knows the man doesn't look fifty let alone fifty-six.

"What other stupid ass reasons do you have to keep us apart?"

I stare into his eyes and decide what the hell, he needs to know this isn't going anywhere. "I'm in the city temporarily. As soon as matters are settled, I'm going home."

"And where's home?"

Crap. This is why I brought up all the other reasons! I don't want him prying into my life. "I can't tell you."

"Can't or won't?"

"Can't."

"If you're in trouble, you can tell me. I can deal with it. I'll make sure you and Ollie are safe."

I shake my head. "We are safe. But if I tell you, there's a chance we aren't safe."

He drops my hand and sags back in his chair. "What the fuck, Faith?"

His use of my given name slices through me. I refuse to think about why. No, I power on.

I stand. "I'm sorry, but this is how it has to be."

I whirl around and rush out of the room. When he doesn't try to stop me, my stomach cramps, and I nearly keel over. The butterflies have all died a grim death.

It's the way it has to be, I repeat to myself.

Chapter 9

I'm addicted to collecting Beatles albums. I need Help! ~ Text from Pops to Hailey

POPS

"What's the difference between a tire and three-hundred-sixty-five used condoms? What's the difference between a pregnant woman and a lightbulb? What's the difference between a Catholic priest and a zit? What's the best part about sex with twenty-eight-year-olds?" Dirty jokes erupt from Barney.

"What is wrong with you?" Hailey asks when he takes a break.

I open my mouth to make up some lie, but she's not talking to me. She's shaking her head and staring at Barney like he's lost his mind. Good. I don't need to discuss the problems in my love life with my daughter.

"Someone," he points to me, "has a fit when I tell dirty jokes when Faith's around. I need to get all the jokes out."

What? I look around the bar. "Faith's here?"

Did she come back? When she ran out of the place this afternoon, I had to lock myself down so I wouldn't follow her. Until I know what's got her running scared, I need to proceed with caution. And chasing after her and forcing her to tell me all her secrets is not cautious.

Hailey rubs her hands together. "I'm dying to hear how lunch went." She wiggles her brows. "Did you finally get through to her? Maybe take her back to your place for some afternoon delight."

Phoebe slaps her arm. "What's wrong with you? He's your father." Her nose wrinkles. "He's not my father, but I don't want to think about him and Faith you know…" She shivers.

Suzie snickers. "Because you consider him your father. Why don't you put the Uncles out of their misery and finally admit Pops is the one you chose to walk you down the aisle?"

Barney's joke vomiting halts, and Lenny, Sid, and Wally move closer to the bar.

Lenny throws an arm over Phoebe's shoulder. "Did you finally come to your senses, Doll?"

Sid elbows him out of the way and yanks Phoebe to his side. "She's going to pick me. After all, I have the most experience with weddings."

Suzie giggles. "I don't think being married five times is the kind of experience she's looking for."

"I told you. It's four times."

"And I told you, common law marriage is still marriage in the eyes of the law," Hailey insists.

I don't know why she bothers. Sid knows damn well and good he's been married five times, but he sure likes to tease my daughter. Doesn't she notice the gleam in his eye? My girl can be stubborn.

"If I promise not to tell any more dirty jokes, will you let me walk you down the aisle?" Barney asks with a flutter of his lashes. I chuckle at how ridiculous he looks.

Wally puts his arm around Phoebe's waist and draws her close. "You ready to admit what we all know? I'm the one walking you down the aisle."

Ryker returns from the restroom and growls when he notices my brothers surrounding his woman. "All of you need to keep your hands off my wife."

Wally doesn't move. "She's not your wife yet."

My brothers laugh at Wally's comment, but I watch Ryker. His nostrils flare as his frustration mounts. He wanted to drag Phoebe to the courthouse for a wedding the day after he asked her to marry him. It's been nine long months of watching him lose his patience.

To his credit, he doesn't lash out at Wally. He takes a step forward and motions to Phoebe. "Princess, come here."

Hailey and Suzie move to block her. "Who you ordering around, big guy?" Suzie asks with her arms crossed over her chest.

Grayson tugs her out of the way. "Stop causing trouble, Precious." Once he's out of the target zone, he smirks at Ryker. "My *wife* didn't mean any harm."

When Aiden steps forward, my daughter snarls at him. "Don't you even think about it."

He raises his hands. "I wouldn't dare, *wife* of mine."

Ryker grunts and motions to Phoebe again.

Phoebe taps Hailey on the shoulder. "What are you doing?"

Hailey rolls her eyes. "Duh. I'm protecting you."

Phoebe raises an eyebrow. "I'm not sure how you missed it, but my protector is standing right in front of you."

"Yeah, yeah, yeah. We all know Ryker is Phoebe's protector. We didn't miss it when he took on her husband. Can we get back to the matter at hand?" Sid asks.

Ryker raises a brow. "What matter at hand?"

Phoebe sighs. "They're pressuring me about who will walk me down the aisle at our wedding."

"Princess." He reaches past Hailey and takes her hand and gathers her in his arms. "Tell them already. You've got enough vodka for the rest of your life. And I'm not buying another dozen vases for all the flowers. What are you waiting for?"

"But it's fun to tease them," she pouts.

Her words make my chest swell with pride. The Phoebe who arrived here last year was a timid mouse who would have never dared to tease my brothers. Watching her come out of her shell has been nothing short of magnificent.

"Darling," I say and pause until she looks my way. "You tease us as long as you want. We're big boys. We can handle it."

She winks at me. There's no need for her wink. I know she picked me. Hell, I've written my speech for the wedding reception already.

The group disperses with the girls and their men going to play pool in the backroom and my brothers heading to their table for some poker, although they hardly ever manage to play more than a few hands. They're usually too busy trash-talking and planning practical jokes on me.

I stop Wally before he can join them. "A word?" I tilt my head toward the hallway.

"It's time," I say once we're inside my office with the door closed behind us.

"Time?" he asks. He knows damn well what I'm talking about.

"You need to use your resources to find out what happened to Faith."

Wally has resources none of us can dream of. While the rest of my brothers retired from the military and government completely, Wally never has. He does freelance work for the government in areas of the world I have no plans to ever revisit. One trip to the Middle East was enough for a lifetime for me.

He crosses his arms over his chest. "Are you sure? You lost your mind last time I tried to pry into her background."

Fuck! I rub a hand over my face. He's going to make me say it out loud. "She won't give me a chance until the situation is resolved."

He shrugs. "Then, move on. Find another woman to warm your bed."

My hand is around his throat before I realize I've moved. "Don't you dare talk about Faith like she's a woman you pick up in a bar and have a one-night stand with. Faith is the one you give up those one-night stands for."

We stay there staring at each other, my hand squeezing his neck, for a minute. Wally isn't bothered by my hand on his throat. We both know if he wanted to, he'd have me on the floor and cuffed within seconds. I flex my hand and release him before stepping back.

I let him go, but I'll be damned if I apologize. No one is talking smack about my woman. And she is my woman. I've claimed her. She just hasn't realized it yet. I'm not worried. I can be patient. I've waited my entire life to find the one. I can wait a little longer.

"Are you sure?" Wally asks. "Didn't you promise her you wouldn't go digging around?"

"Fuck!" I can't break my promise to her. But wait a minute. I promised I wouldn't let Wally dig into her past. I never promised I wouldn't. Wally may have resources I can't tap into, but he's not the only person I know who has access to those resources. I need to make some calls.

"She won't thank you," he points out as if he can read my mind, which he can. When you've been on the type of missions together that we have, you learn to read your teammate without a word being spoken.

"She'll get over it. Especially if Ollie is safe."

"You think the kid is involved somehow?"

"Yeah," I say and explain. "It's the way she looks at him. Like she knows someone is coming for him, but she's determined to stand in their way come hell or high water."

"I've seen the look." He removes his phone from his pocket. "I got this."

"No. I promised I wouldn't let you dig around. But I never promised I wouldn't do any digging around of my own."

Wally chuckles. "Leave it to Max to find a loophole. I'm sending you a contact. I'll let him know to expect your call."

"Thanks, brother." I slap his back.

"You got it bad, brother. You in love?"

I open my arms wide. "I'm not trying to hide it."

He slaps my back. "Happy for you."

"I gotta get her shit sorted first."

He grins. "You will. And if you don't, there's a table of brothers out there ready and willing to help. All you have to do is say the word."

"Thanks." I open the door. "In the meantime, I've got a business to run."

I step into the hallway and notice Hailey and her friends waiting at the end of the hall.

Hailey's shoulders hunch in disappointment when she sees us. "They were doing serious stuff. No show today."

"Your girl's crazy," Wally says as he passes me.

Yeah, and I couldn't be prouder.

Chapter 10

As a kid I wondered why my parents were always in a bad mood. Now, I'm like 'Oooohhh'.

"Sorry, I'm late," I say as I rush into *You Cheat, We Eat* on Tuesday morning. "Ollie forgot his math homework and I had to go back to the apartment to fetch it for him. And then his homework wasn't where he said it would be. Why would it be? I finally found it underneath his cereal bowl he neglected to pick up this morning. A cereal bowl I discovered was most definitely not empty like I thought it was when I picked it up. Long story short I had to change my outfit before I could drive back to the school with his homework."

I finally stop my word vomiting and look up to notice Hailey, Phoebe, and Suzie lounging in the reception area. Huh. Why is Suzie here? She called me and begged me to work for her today. I look around at the group and my suspicions rise. The expectant looks on their faces along with the sparkling in their eyes does not bode well for me.

"I thought you had a bottling emergency," I say to Suzie.

"More like a 'my stocks are low, and I have a huge order to fill'-emergency."

"Where's Ryker?" Maybe he'll save me from this obvious girl talk ambush.

"He's out chasing a skip. He'll be home before Friday," Phoebe says.

Suzie snickers. "Yeah, because he wants to be home for your bachelorette party."

"Your soon-to-be husband is attending your bachelorette party?"

I've heard of joint bachelor/bachelorette parties, but I don't see the point. It's not really a bachelorette party then, is it? How are you supposed to get drunk and dance all night with men who are not your fiancé if your fiancé is there? Not like I did that. Okay, I did, but it was only the one man, and he was more interested in my best friend Valerie than me, so it doesn't count.

Phoebe giggles and shakes her head.

Hailey joins her giggling. "Can you imagine?"

I'm lost and confused, but it's fine. These ladies have been friends for a while. I'm the intruder here, not them.

I hang up my coat and clap my hands. "Alrighty. Time to work. What do you need me to do today?"

"Have a seat." Hailey points to an empty chair. "We got you a coffee. I hope you like mocha lattes."

"If it has chocolate in it, I'll drink it," I declare before grabbing the mug. I take a sip and let the warm liquid fortify me for whatever is coming.

"Can we get a move on? I need to get my brew on," Suzie says.

Yep. I knew this was an ambush the minute I walked in here.

"Why don't you want to be with my dad?" Hailey asks, and I nearly choke on my sip of chocolate coffee deliciousness.

"Did you not hear me when I told you about my morning? I'm a single mom. I don't have time to date."

Suzie stands. "Mystery solved. I'm out of here." She sets her coffee down on the desk except she misses the desk, and the to-go cup falls to the ground and coffee bursts everywhere.

I stand and rush to the bathroom where I gather a bunch of paper towels. I'm back and mopping up the mess before the others have moved.

"She's got mad mom skills," Suzie points out.

"And you've got mad klutzy skills," Hailey says.

When the mess is cleaned up, Suzie takes off to 'get her brew on' and I sit behind the reception desk to confront the pile of documents needing filing. How did all these documents manage to pile up in the past week?

"Nuh-uh." Hailey slaps her hands on top of the documents I'm trying to sort. "We're not done with our conversation."

I tilt my head like I'm confused. I'm not, but it's worth a try. "We're not?"

"No. You need to explain why having a fifteen-year-old son who seems pretty self-sufficient if you ask me prevents you from dating my dad."

"Maybe she's not into Pops," Phoebe suggests.

Hailey gasps. "You're kidding, right? Have you seen my dad? He's a total silver fox."

Phoebe's nose scrunches up. "Will you stop talking about your dad like he's a man? It's disturbing."

"My dad is a man. He's got all the man parts and everything."

Phoebe feigns gagging. "Stop. Please stop."

"You're weird." Hailey returns her attention to me. "Anyway, we've established my dad is hot, you're hot. What's the problem?"

"Did you not hear the part about me being a single mom and being way too busy for a man?"

Hailey scoffs. "Please. Other single women date and get re-married. Why not you?"

"Are you trying to pimp your dad out?"

She rolls her eyes. "Duh. I want him to be happy. He looks at you like you hang the moon."

Phoebe nods. "It is pretty romantic."

I point to myself. "Single mom." And in Milwaukee temporarily, but I don't mention the last part. The information will bring up questions I have no intention of answering.

"This is why I'm hesitant to have children," Phoebe says.

"You don't want to have children?"

"It's not like I had the best example of parents, and Ryker is an orphan. Neither one of us would know what we're doing."

"Trust me, no parent knows what they're doing."

"You seem to have your shit together."

"It's the single parent thing," Hailey answers on my behalf. "My dad was the same way. I don't know what he was like when I wasn't around, but in my presence, my dad always looked like he had it together."

"I'm pretty sure Ollie knows I don't have it together." I clear my throat. "Anyway, do you want children?" I ask Phoebe.

She gets this dreamy look on her face. "Little babies who look like Ryker? Who wouldn't?"

"Then, do it. Don't worry about parenting. Every parent screws up a million times. I can't tell you how many times I've told myself I'm ruining my kid's life."

She bites her lip. "I don't know. It's scary."

Hailey chuckles. "Scarier than kidnappings and ex-husbands who want to lock you up?"

Husbands who want to lock you up? Obviously, Wally didn't tell me everything about Phoebe's past. Yikes.

"Look," I tell Phoebe, "don't let fear stop you. If you want children, talk to Ryker about your fears."

The phone rings, and I answer it. By the time I finish the call, Phoebe and Hailey have moved off to their offices. Phew. I've survived the inquisition portion of the workday.

The day passes quickly until Ollie arrives at four. Hailey asked if he could come over to walk her dogs. I couldn't say no – not when she asked while I was facetiming with Ollie and he heard. Guessing by the wink she gave him, she knew exactly what she was doing.

I stand to greet him with a hug. He pushes me away. "Ma, don't embarrass me."

Ugh. He's definitely entering the 'my mom embarrasses me by existing'-phase. "There's no one here," I say, and then to annoy him mess with his hair.

Hailey comes out of her office with her dogs in tow. "Thanks for coming to walk my dogs, Ollie." She hands him the leads. "This is Lola, and this is Leroy."

Ollie drops to his knees to let the dogs sniff him. Once they've approved of him, he rubs them down. They attack him with kisses, and he giggles. I soak in the sound. It's been a while since I've heard my boy giggle like the fifteen-year-old he is. He's always somber and out to save the world. It's exhausting.

"Don't go too far," I order as he gets ready to leave.

He rolls his eyes. "Yes, Bossy Mom."

"Do they ever snap out of the sarcastic phase?" I ask the room.

Phoebe giggles. "Judging by Hailey, the answer is no."

"Hey! Sarcasm is an art form."

I know Ollie is fifteen and the area the PI firm is located in is safe, but I still worry the entire time he's walking the dogs. I'm relieved when he returns forty-five minutes later wearing all the clothes he left in and towing two now tired dogs behind him.

"There's a dog park five blocks away," he says as he lets the dogs loose. They immediately run to Phoebe's office.

"No. Get out of here. No peeing! And you, no humping!" This I gotta see.

Leroy is sniffing around Phoebe's desk looking for all intents and purposes like he's going to lift up a leg and pee on it despite just returning from a walk, while Lola is trying to jump on Phoebe who's holding her off for all she's worth.

Hailey stomps into the room. She takes Lola by the collar and drags her away from Phoebe. "No humping Phoebe. Bad dog." Lola whines as Hailey pushes her out of the room. Once Lola is taken care of, she returns for Leroy. "No peeing on Phoebe's desk." She grabs him by the neck, and he barks and takes off. "Sorry, Phoebe. I thought once Suzie stopped spraying the puppy pee stuff on your desk, he'd stop peeing here."

"Can we get a dog, Ma?" Ollie asks once the chaos settles down.

Lucky for me, but unlucky for him, I'm prepared for his question. "We don't have a yard for a dog. It would be cruel to have a dog without a yard for him to run around in."

"What about when we have a yard? Can we have a dog then?"

"Maybe."

He grunts. "Maybe means no."

Maybe totally means no, but being a mom means being willing to lie to your children. It's for their own good. "No, maybe means ask me when we have a yard, and we can talk about it then."

I gather my coat and purse. "Come on. Let's get home. You've got homework and I need to make dinner."

"I'm starving."

"Of course, you are."

Ollie would eat me out of house and home if he had the chance. Teenagers. The unfortunate consequence of adorable babies.

Chapter 11

That awkward moment when you're not sure if you actually have free time, or if you're forgetting something.

I MOAN WHEN THERE's a knock on the door on Friday night. I've barely managed to sit down on the sofa for a moment of peace. Ollie is spread out next to me playing a game on his laptop with his headset on. I was planning to search for that bottle of wine I know I hid in the kitchen cabinets somewhere and watch a mind-numbing movie.

I press pause on my 'relaxing with a bottle of wine Friday night'-plans and force myself to my feet and shuffle to the door. When I look through the peephole, I see Phoebe, Suzie, and Hailey waving at me. Is it too late to switch off all the lights and pretend I'm not home?

"Open the door!" Hailey orders. "We can see your shadow. We know you're there." Like father, like daughter.

I open the door and motion for them to come in. "What's going on?" I ask once they're inside with the door closed behind them to prevent Mrs. Lebowski from getting any good gossip about my life.

"It's my bachelorette party!" Phoebe shouts. She's wearing a pink t-shirt with the words *Brews before I do's* stamped on it.

"Um, congratulations?" Her statement doesn't exactly explain what they're doing here.

"You're coming with us," Phoebe declares.

I shake my head but don't get any words out before she's insisting, "You're coming and that's that."

I'm surprised she doesn't stomp her foot. On the other hand, I can't see Ms. Perfect stomping her foot. If she weren't so darn nice, I'd hate her for how put together and gorgeous she is.

"I'm too old for a bachelorette party," I protest.

Hailey huffs. "You're forty-five, not sixty." I sure feel sixty right now looking at their young wrinkle-free faces.

"You have to come. I had a t-shirt made for you and everything." Suzie holds up a blue t-shirt with the words *Bride's Brew Crew* stamped on it.

"Go already, Ma," Ollie says from the sofa.

"Will you—"

He cuts me off. "I'll be fine. I won't have a party. I won't invite anyone over. And I'll be in bed by midnight."

"Midnight?" I raise an eyebrow. His bedtime is eleven on Friday nights, and he knows it.

"It was worth a try."

Suzie shoves the t-shirt into my hands. "Here, go get changed. Apparently, we have somewhere to be."

"You don't know where we're going?"

She huffs. "No one would tell me."

Hailey giggles. "Because your reaction is going to be awesome!"

I know a lost cause when I hear it. I rush off to get changed. Five minutes later, I'm dressed in clean jeans and have managed to brush my hair out and add a bit of make-up to my face.

"Come on," Hailey says when I enter the living room. "The uber is waiting for us."

Fifteen minutes later, we arrive at an art gallery. "What are we doing here?" Suzie asks as she looks around the street.

"We're going to a paint and sip party!" Hailey announces in a loud voice.

"I guess that explains why you asked me to pack drinks for everyone," Suzie says as she hauls a large bag out of the car.

"I love this idea!" Phoebe shouts.

"I have to ask. How many shots did you give her already?"

Hailey holds up two fingers in response to my question. "She's a lightweight."

"I don't understand how paint and sip translates to bachelorette party," Suzie whines as we walk into the gallery.

We follow the signs to the back room where the event is taking place. Suzie freezes when we round the corner. She looks back at me. "Oh yeah, now I get it." She wiggles her eyebrows.

What is she wiggling about? I look around and my eyes fall on the poster advertising tonight's activity. Sexy paint night? I look further and notice a man standing in a robe.

Phoebe jumps up and down and claps. "Yeah!"

Hailey raises her hand and high-fives Phoebe. "I totally rock at giving bachelorette parties."

Suzie rolls her eyes before finding four chairs clumped together in a corner of the room and making her way there. She opens her bag and empties the contents out on one of the little tables next to the empty canvasses. She brings out beer, a bottle of vodka, a bottle of vermouth, a cocktail glass, two beer mugs, a bottle of wine, and a wine glass. When she's finished, it looks like we have our own mini-bar.

"My turn," Hailey says before starting to empty her bag. She places a cutting board on the table before adding cheese, sausage, and crackers.

Phoebe throws her arms in the air. "Best bachelorette party ever!"

Hailey leans close to me. "Ask me about my party some time. It was pretty awesome." She looks at Phoebe who's doing some kind of dance in place. "She got drunk then, too."

Suddenly, I'm whirled around by Phoebe. "Oh my god, I didn't invite you to my wedding. I'm a horrible person."

Hailey rolls her eyes before she helps to disentangle me from Phoebe. "It's fine, Phoebe. She's Pops' plus one."

My eyes nearly pop out of my face, and my jaw drops to the ground. "I'm not his plus one."

She bumps me with her hip. "You totally are."

A woman in a multi-colored kaftan claps her hands to gain everyone's attention. When the talking dies down, she begins, "I'm Meadow, and I'm here to welcome you to our sexy paint night." The group cheers. Apparently, Phoebe's not the only woman who already commenced with the sipping portion of the night. Meadow waits for the cheers to quiet down before giving us instructions on how to draw the male figure. I hope no one expects me to actually be able to draw. I have zero artistic ability.

"Here," Suzie says and hands me a glass of wine. "This should help you paint better."

I gulp half of the drink down in one go. I need all the help I can get. I notice Phoebe tottering on her chair with a martini in her hands.

Suzie leans close to whisper. "Don't worry. I watered down her drink. She'll sober up in no time."

Hailey shoves the platter of food into Phoebe's face. "This should help, too."

"Now, let's begin," Meadow says, and the model moves into the middle of the room and drops his robe and strikes a pose.

My grip on my wine glass tightens, and I gulp. "Oh my. Is he?"

"He's a shower, not a grower," Suzie explains.

"I thought the whole shower not a grower thing was made up by romance novels."

She motions to the model. "Obviously not."

"Eh." Phoebe shrugs. "Ryker's bigger."

Hailey giggles. "She's going to regret saying those words in the morning."

"In the morning?" Suzie snorts. "I plan to use the information to embarrass her every chance I get for the rest of her life."

Phoebe is undeterred. It seems martinis shut off her brain to mouth filter. "How about Aiden? He looks like he packs a big meat sandwich down there."

Hailey nabs her drink. "You're cut off."

Phoebe pouts. "Why? Suzie asks all the time, and you don't steal her drinks."

I hand Phoebe my wine. If this is what she says while tipsy, I want to hear more. She takes a sip and her lip curls. "Ugh. Wine. Where's my vodka?"

Hailey gives up and hands her back her drink. "Fine. Don't blame me when you have a massive hangover tomorrow."

"I'm supposed to have a hangover," she slurs. "It's my party!"

"Do you think the model's single?" Suzie asks.

"Why? You're married. Or did you forget?" Silas liked to forget he was married to me all the time. Whether it was jumping in bed with another woman or not remembering Ollie's soccer game, he did the whole forgetting thing a lot.

Suzie grins at me. "I know. I've found my before anyone else."

"Hey, Suzie! How big is Grayson's meat rocket?" Phoebe poses her question loud enough for the entire room to hear her. "He's not very tall, but he's broad. How does that translate in the downstairs department?"

Suzie isn't embarrassed. I don't think she does embarrassed. She points at Phoebe with her paintbrush and paint flies everywhere. I hope this is water-soluble paint. I don't need Ollie asking why I have paint in my hair.

"Don't you worry," Suzie says as she ignores the paint dripping from her brush. "Grayson has no problems in the size department."

Meadow walks over and I expect her to berate us, but there's a smile on her face. "Having fun, ladies?"

We bob our heads in agreement as she looks at Phoebe's canvas. "Um, this is a very modernist take on the male nude form."

I look around my canvas to see hers. There are streaks of black paint on it. That's it. Nothing else. "Actually," Phoebe says while sounding remarkably sober, "it's more of a post-modernist approach."

"Hmmm…" Meadow hums and walks away without looking at the rest of our work.

"How did she act sober one minute after nearly falling off her chair?" I ask Suzie.

She shrugs. "It's her superpower. She grew up a spoiled little rich girl."

There's nothing spoiled about the woman giggling as she splotches paint onto her canvas now.

My thoughts are proved right when Phoebe opens her mouth again. "Do you think Pops has a big joystick?"

Beer erupts from Suzie's mouth as she barks out a laugh. "Oh, she is definitely regretting those words."

"We can talk about Pops and relationships. We can tease Faith about getting it on with him. But one thing we will not do is discuss my father's physical attributes," Hailey lays down the law.

"Sorry." Phoebe hiccups. "He's very yummy to look at." She leans over her chair to look me in the eye. "You really should take him for a ride. I bet it would be the best ride of your life."

My body tingles and warmth spreads through my middle at her words. I'm positive Pops would rock my world. Too bad I will not be buying a ticket for that ride.

Chapter 12

Ninety percent of parenting is wondering when
you can lie down again.

I'm back at work cleaning at McGraw's Pub Monday morning. I'm happy I had the weekend to recover from my hangover
after Friday night. Although Ollie's soccer game was not fun
on Saturday. Deb claimed she had the perfect hangover cure. I
should have known better than to take a sip from her thermos.
My esophagus burned from the amount of vodka she put in
her 'coffee'. These day-afters are why I don't drink often. Add
Ollie's tendency to fall and need a trip to the emergency room
whenever I've had more than one glass of wine and I've nearly
become a teetotaler.

Pops walks into the back room of the pub where I'm wiping
down the edges of the pool table. Can't anyone use a coaster?
Or maybe not let their beer spill everywhere?

"You ready for your coffee break?" Pops asks.

He doesn't need to ask twice. I drop my rag. "Yes."

We've been avoiding each other since the 'date' Hailey instigated under false pretenses last Sunday. Actually, I'm lying. I've
been avoiding Pops like the coward I am. He's asked me to have

coffee every day I was at the pub last week and I came up with excuses each and every time. But I'm too tired this morning to make up some lie.

Pops places his hand on my lower back and gently leads me to a table where two take-out coffees are sitting. "I got you one of those fancy mocha coffees you like."

I narrow my eyes at him. "How do you know I like mocha coffee?"

"I have eyes. I see the way you suck down coffee and chocolate. Plus, I've been where you are – raising a single child on my own. Caffeine is a must-have in every parent's diet."

I take a sip of my coffee and my eyes close as I moan. This is some good coffee. When I open my eyes again, Pops is staring at me with heat in his eyes. I feel my cheeks warm, and I glance away.

Pops clears his throat. "We need to talk."

"Can it wait?" Until never, I think but know better than to say.

"It has to do with Ollie."

Now, he has my attention. "Is something wrong? Did the school call? Or someone else?"

"It's the someone else we need to talk about."

I narrow my eyes at him. "I told you. I can't tell you what happened."

He reaches across the table and grasps my hand. "Spitfire, I know what happened."

I study him. Is he lying? Is this some trick to get me to spill the truth? He stares back at me, the honesty clear to see in his eyes. Damnit. My stomach rolls. This can't be good.

I yank my hand from his. "How? You promised not to go digging around."

He clears his throat. "Actually, I promised I wouldn't let Wally dig around. And I didn't."

"Semantics. You knew I didn't want anyone digging around." I should stand up and march right out of here. He lied to me. But I can't move. There's a big part of me relieved to have someone else who knows the story. Not even my best friend knows the whole truth. I couldn't risk her sticking her nose where it didn't belong. And she would have. Valerie is fearless.

"I am not letting someone I care about be in danger. What kind of man would I be then?"

I snarl because I'm not quite ready to let things go. "Maybe I'm not interested in the kind of man you are."

"Spitfire, don't lie to yourself or me. It demeans both of us." He reaches for my hand again, but I cross my arms over my chest to keep my hands out of his reach.

"What do you know?" Maybe he doesn't know everything. Maybe I'm blowing everything out of proportion. And maybe I'll win the lottery tomorrow.

"I know Ollie is a brave boy you should be proud of having raised right."

Hell. He does know everything. My arms loosen, and my head falls forehead in defeat.

"I know the FBI are assholes for not putting you in Witsec."

"Actually, the U.S. Marshals are in charge of the Witsec program," I say to be contradictory.

Pops grins and moves on. "I know you can't return to Saint Louis because the situation there is volatile." He doesn't stop talking and rocking my world. "I know you moved here and, with an abundance of caution, changed your name."

"Abundance of caution? You don't think we need to hide?" Can I go home? Can I stop hiding?

"I don't think the gang is still looking for Ollie, but it's safer if you stay here." He pauses to take a deep breath. "Do you want to tell me the whole story?"

There's no sense keeping my mouth shut anymore. He knows the gist of it anyway. I take a long sip of my coffee before beginning.

"Ollie has always been a crusader, fighting for the underdog. I think he gets it from his dad." At Pops' raised eyebrow, I explain. "Not like you think. Silas was a bully." He growls. "I didn't let him bully us around, but he never stopped trying. I think it opened Ollie's eyes to how tough it can be for people who are marginalized."

"Your kid is pretty awesome."

Pride blossoms in my chest and I can't keep the smile from my face. "Yeah, he is."

"Anyway, Ollie was walking home one day after school and saw a crowd gathering. Of course, he had to go check it out. What he saw..." I trail off. This is the hard part.

Pops stands and moves his chair next to mine. He places one arm around my shoulders and gathers me near. I take a moment to appreciate the comfort he's offering. It's been a long time since someone comforted me. I'm usually the one offering comfort, not the other way around.

"There was a group of five teenage boys. They had a woman. No, not a woman. A girl on the ground. They'd ripped her shirt open and were trying to get her pants off. She was fighting them, but she wasn't going to win. And the crowd? They stood there and watched as a girl was sexually violated. My son has no fear. He walked right up to the girl and took her hand and helped her to her feet. Once she was standing, he told her to run. She didn't hesitate. Ollie was ready to fight those kids all on his own, but the rest of the crowd finally woke up and helped. The members of the group, who were pledging to become gang members, were beat up and humiliated."

"Was Ollie hurt?"

I shake my head. "He was fine. He told me what happened when I came home from work, but I didn't think much of it. I assumed it was over. The girl was safe."

When I don't continue, Pops squeezes my shoulder. "What happened?"

"We were targeted. It started small. Kids following me in the grocery store, saying nasty stuff. I didn't care. I wasn't going to give in to a bunch of bullies."

"A gang is not a bunch of bullies."

I raise an eyebrow. "They're not?"

He sighs. "Okay, they are. But they're more. They're violent and dangerous."

"Yes." I swallow. "I learned that the hard way."

"What happened?" he asks again.

"They stuck knives in the tires of my car. And then they threw a brick through our front window."

"What did the police say?"

"There wasn't much they could do. There were no witnesses, of course. And Ollie couldn't describe the would-be rapists except to say what gang colors they were wearing. There was no way for us to get protection. Instead, Agent Judson offered to change our names and get us out of the area until things calmed down."

"Which is how you ended up here?"

I nod.

"My sources claim no one's actively looking for Ollie, but there is concern your return would light a powder keg."

I frown. It's the same thing Judson has been saying for months.

He places a finger under my chin and lifts my head. "Don't worry. I'll figure out a way to solve the problem and get you home."

"You will? You're a pub owner. What can you possibly do?"

He grins. "I have more brothers than the ones who play poker here."

I need to make a decision. Let him wade in and hope he can help us or tell him to back off. What choice do I have? It's not like he'll back off if I tell him to anyway.

I swallow the lump in my throat along with my pride. "Thank you for your help." He grins, but I raise a hand before he can celebrate his little victory. "But please be careful. I don't want anyone else hurt."

"You worried about me, Spitfire?"

I roll my eyes. "Don't read into it. I worry about everyone. It's my job. I'm a mom."

"Since I know all about your secrets, you're out of excuses. I think it's time we went on a date," Pops declares.

My stomach goes crazy like I'm a freshman and my senior crush just said hi to me in the hallway. "Nothing's changed. I'm still leaving when the situation in Saint Louis is resolved."

"Yes, but from what I've heard, it could take months. In the meantime, we date." He raises an eyebrow. "Or do you have another list of excuses for me to deal with first?"

I'm sure if I did come up with a bunch of problems, he wouldn't hesitate to solve them. I guess we're going out on a date.

I hold up my finger. "One date. I'm agreeing to one date. Nothing more."

"Works for me," he mumbles before he inches closer to me and his lips find mine. It's a sweet kiss, a brief touching of the lips. It ends nearly before it begins, but my lips tingle. I don't think my lips have ever tingled before. Maybe this date isn't a good idea after all.

"No way." He shakes his head. "You're not backing out now."

Him being able to read my mind does not bode well for me. Although I guess in certain instances, his mindreading could come in handy. An image of him between my legs pops in my head and an ache grows down below.

Pops stands and hauls me to my feet. "Come on. You need to get back to work. If we follow where your train of thought is going, we'll be hurrying things and I have no intention of rushing things with you. No, I want to take my time."

He pats my butt, and I squeak before running off. He's right. We need to take things slow, and if I don't get out of his space, I'm going to jump him. *One date, Faith. One date.* And now I'm lying to myself. The man makes me crazy.

Chapter 13

I'm all for being a mom and doing everything for my kid but planning dinner every night for eighteen years seems excessive.

BY THE TIME SUNDAY morning rolls around – the day of the big date – I'm a nervous wreck. Of course, I am. I haven't been on a date since Silas and I were dating. And I'm not sure what Silas and I did could be considered dating. It's not like the guy ever took me out for a romantic dinner. Oh god, is Pops going to take me to a bar to hang out with his friends? No. I shake my head. He's not stupid. Or is he?

"Ma!" Ollie shouts.

My mouth automatically forms the words "No shouting," without me thinking about it.

He snorts. "Like you would have noticed me mid-freak out any other way."

"I am not freaking out." I lie. I'm totally freaking out. Did I choose the right outfit? Pops said to dress warm. Where can we possibly be going, which requires dressing warm? I thought we'd get a bite to eat. Isn't the first date always a meal? And now I'm wondering if I should eat before he arrives in case he doesn't feed me. Ugh. Why is dating this hard?

The doorbell rings and ends my fantasy of climbing out my bedroom window and escaping for the afternoon to an insane asylum. Ollie jumps up from his seat at the kitchen table where he's doing his homework and rushes to the door.

"Ollie," I warn him, but I'm too late, he's already opening the door.

"What did I say about opening the door to strangers?"

Ollie rolls his eyes. "It's Pops. He's not a stranger."

"Hi, Ollie," Pops says. He winks at me. "Hey, Spitfire."

"Come in," I say and motion him inside with a sweep of my arm.

He produces a bouquet of flowers he was hiding behind his back. "These are for you."

I melt at the gesture. I love when a man brings a woman flowers, and I don't care what that says about me as a woman. I can be a feminist and still love getting flowers, right? "Thank you," I say and snatch the flowers from his hands. "I'll put these in water."

Ollie laughs. "Ma loves all the romantic stuff. She'll probably stare at those flowers like a million times this week."

My face heats with mortification. "Ollie! Shush!"

"What? It's true."

Lord save me from teenage boys.

"What about you?" Pops asks Ollie. "Your mom said you like to play video games." I look up from my flowers to see him retrieve a package from his coat. "This is for you."

Ollie stares at the gift for a long moment before curiosity gets the better of him and he grabs it. He rips open the packaging. "This is the latest game. This is really cool."

"Ollie, what do you say?"

My boy straightens up. "Thank you." He holds out his hand and shakes Pops'. Of course, he has to ruin it the next second when he drops to the floor and yanks his game console out from under the couch where I hid it this morning while cleaning. We've officially lost him.

I finish putting the flowers in my one and only vase and set them on the kitchen table. Pops walks over to stand next to me. "They're gorgeous. Thank you," I gush because inside I'm all girly girl.

"You ready?" he asks as he takes my hand and leads me to the door.

Ollie is already in his own little world with his game. "Ollie!" He doesn't listen. "Ollie!" I shout again and kick his foot for good measure.

He scowls and looks up at me. I point to the kitchen table. "I'll be home for dinner. No playing your game until your history paper and math homework is done."

"Yes, Bossy Mom."

Pops growls, and I pat his chest to assure him it's fine. Big – no, gigantic – mistake. His muscles bunch where I touch him, and I can feel how warm he is. And now all I can think about is ripping his flannel shirt off and touching his skin. *One date, Faith. One date.*

"Son," Pops starts, but I cut him off.

"It's fine. He'll listen and do his homework like I asked."

Ollie puts away his game and stomps to the kitchen table where his homework is spread out. "I'm going already."

I take my coat from the hook on the wall next to the door and Pops helps me into it. The butterflies in my stomach don't flap their wings. No, they're swooning over his romantic gesture. They're not the only ones. I need to be on guard with this man.

Once we're settled in Pops' truck, he switches on the engine and we head out. "Where are we going?" I ask when I notice the city is behind us.

"It's a surprise, but trust me, you're going to like it."

"How do you know I'm going to like it? You hardly know me."

Pops reaches across the center console to take my hand in his. "Spitfire, I know you. I know you like romantic gestures like flowers. I know you're a fierce mom who knows to pick her battles. I know you'll do anything to make this world a better place for your son."

"Enough." I tug on my hand, but he doesn't let go.

He stops talking, and we settle into silence for the rest of the drive. I wish I could say it's awkward silence, and I'm fidgeting in my seat. Unfortunately, it's not. It's comfortable as we drive with Pops holding my hand and rubbing circles in my skin. And those aren't goosebumps. I'm cold is all.

When Pops turns off of the highway and onto a secondary road, I look around and notice signs for an apple orchard. I sit up in my seat. "Are we going apple picking?"

He chuckles. "If you want. I brought a picnic basket for lunch, but I thought we'd figure out what else we want to do while we're here. In addition to apple picking, there are hayrides, and there's a tour of the cider making."

I squeal in excitement. I'm not from Wisconsin. I've never been to an apple orchard before. "I tried to get Ollie to go apple picking with me, but he refused. He's 'too old' for apple picking."

"I'll go apple picking all day long with you," Pops promises in a deep voice. I'm not sure he's talking about apple picking anymore. I shiver and my stomach tingles. Oh boy is this man dangerous.

He drives into the parking lot and finds a spot. "Stay there," he says when I grasp the door handle after he switches the engine off.

I watch as he hops out and strolls around the front of the truck to my door and opens it. He doesn't hold out a hand for me. No, his hands squeeze my waist, and he lifts me out of my seat before placing me on my feet.

"Are you going to be romantic all day?" I snap to hide how my skin is tingling from his touch.

He bends forward and places his lips against my forehead before responding. "I plan to be romantic for as long as you let me."

My knees buckle, and I hold onto his shirt to stop myself from falling at his feet. This man should come with a warning label – *Warning! Extremely dangerous. Can cause instantaneous combustion of ovaries.*

"Do you want to eat now or pick apples first?"

Good. A change of subject. I bounce on my toes. "Apples first."

"All right." He takes my hand. "I'll come back for the picnic basket."

I have to stop myself from skipping as we walk to the entrance where we are given baskets for our apples and instructions on how to pick apples without harming the trees or nature.

"How did you come up with the idea of an apple orchard?" I ask as we stroll through the apple trees.

His cheeks pinken. "I might have had help."

"I'm assuming Hailey since your buddies would have sent us to a shooting range."

"Actually, it was Phoebe. Hailey suggested a play. My daughter and her drama." He shakes his head. From what I've heard, Hailey was quite the drama geek in high school and insisted on majoring in drama at college. Pops supported her despite worrying about the lack of job opportunities for drama majors. "And Suzie wanted me to take you on a brewery tour."

I stop and whirl around to look up at him. "Exactly how many people were involved in putting together our date?"

He clears his throat. "It wasn't my idea. They converged on me at the pub while I was bartending and couldn't escape."

"Everyone seems to be all up in everyone else's business in your group of friends." I try to sound annoyed, but really I'm trying to cover up my jealousy. My friends back home didn't hang out together all the time and act more like a family than friends. Except for Valerie, my friends didn't spend much time at my house or hanging out with Ollie at all. Man, I miss Valerie.

As for my family, there's only my parents left, and they retired to Alaska. They went on an Alaskan cruise when Ollie was three years old and fell in love with the place. They moved there the next year and haven't looked back. They offered to return to Saint Louis when I kicked Silas out after Ollie's ninth birthday, but I couldn't let them. They're happy and living the life they always dreamed of.

Pops bumps my shoulder. "You'll get used to it." Which is exactly what I'm afraid of.

After we pick apples, I'm starving. Max takes the apples to his truck and returns with a picnic basket. We find a quiet place to spread out the blanket and have our lunch. I'm not surprised when he removes container after container of mouth-watering food. The man does own a pub with a kitchen after all.

"Everything looks yummy, Pops."

He growls before placing a finger under my chin to lift my head. He leans in close before declaring, "I told you. You don't call me Pops. You call me Max."

"What's the big deal?"

His finger moves from my chin to palm my neck. He squeezes my neck and drags me closer. "The difference," he whispers, "is I don't want you calling me Pops when I'm touching you. I want to hear you sigh my name."

"Max," I start.

"Yep, just like that." His head dips, and his lips claim mine. His tongue darts out and licks my bottom lip. I lose my mind and open my mouth to allow my tongue to duel with his. Before I know what's happening, I'm laying on my back on the blanket with Max hovering above me feasting from my mouth like he's on a mission to taste every single inch of space.

He ends the kiss, and I mewl in disappointment. He smirks. "Later. First, I need to feed you." My stomach rumbles in agreement.

"I could get used to this," I say as I fall back to lay on the blanket once I've eaten my weight in food.

Max lays down next to me, places his arm around my shoulders, and hauls me near. I snuggle right up to him. "If you're trying to scare me, it isn't working. I want you to get used to having me in your life."

Instead of me scaring him off, he's scaring the snot out of me. "I said one date," I remind him.

"What are you afraid of?"

Everything. The way my body heats after a single touch from him. How I can't stop thinking about him like I'm a hormonal teenager when he's not near. The hope I feel about the future when he's around. There's a lot to be scared of.

"Take a chance, sweetheart. I promise I'll make it worth your and Ollie's while."

The inclusion of Ollie is what short circuits my brain and has me agreeing before I can stop myself.

"Yeah?" He asks.

I bob my head like an idiot. This man can destroy me, and I just handed him the key.

Chapter 14

My kid is turning out just like me. Well played, karma. Well played.

LIKE THE IDIOT I am, I continue to make bad decisions for the rest of the day. Case in point? Max hardly has to work at it before he manages to convince me to join him at the pub for dinner. We've spent most of the day together, but I'm not ready to say good-bye. I call Ollie to ask him to join us at the pub, but he's not interested.

When I hang up, I bite my fingernail in worry.

Max tugs my finger away from my mouth. "He's fine, sweetheart. He's fifteen. He can spend a day alone."

"I know he *can* spend the day alone, but I don't want him to have to. Weekends are family time. I should go home and spend the evening with him." There's no doubt about it. I'm not getting any single mom points leaving him alone all day.

He pulls the truck over. "If you want to go home, say the word and I'll take you there. But you know he's playing his new video game and is perfectly fine."

Darn. I hate when he's right. I wish I could yell at him that he has no idea what he's talking about, but of course, he does.

He was a single dad after all. And why does he have to be this considerate? Can't he be an asshole for a minute or two to allow my obsession with him to cool off? He's really not playing fair.

I let out a breath of air. "Fine. Let's go have dinner."

Max takes my hand as we walk into the pub. I tug on my hand, but he doesn't budge. "I'm not going to hide or lie about our relationship."

"I'm not trying to hide or lie. I don't like the attention is all." And I'm not lying. I know the second we walk in there, his buddies are going to commence teasing him. They may be in their fifties, but they sure don't act like adults.

We walk into the pub and, sure enough, cheers erupt.

"About time!"

"We knew you could do it, Pops!"

"Does part B fit into slot A?"

At Barney's question, Max drops my hand and stalks over to the group. "I will not have you making fun of Faith and making her feel uncomfortable." He glowers at them until they nod in agreement. "I'm not afraid to ban your asses from my place."

Barney holds up his hands. "Whoa. There's no need to get hasty."

"Apologize to the lady," Max orders.

I wait in the doorway and watch as the former soldiers stand and approach me. I'm sure my eyes are the size of saucers by the time they reach me. Max walks around them and places an arm around my shoulder, making it clear whose side he's on.

"We're sorry!" They declare in unison like a bunch of teenagers who got caught sneaking into the girl's locker room.

I'm surprised none of them twists their foot or bats their eyelashes.

I grunt. "Fine. You're forgiven."

They whoop. Barney yanks me out of Max's arms to twirl me around. Max growls and steals me back. "I'm not a toy," I scold but I'm laughing.

"Stop hogging her," Suzie says and takes my hand. "The girls are over here." She drags me to the table where she's sitting with Hailey and Phoebe.

"Um, I'm here to have dinner with Max."

"Ooooh, it's Max now, is it?" Suzie wiggles her eyebrows, and I wonder if it's too late to have Max drive me home.

Hailey leans close and whispers, "We wanted to get you out of the danger zone. After the last prank from Pops on Wally, I'm sure this prank is going to be epic."

Max sets a glass of red wine in front of me. "Sorry, sweetheart. I need to check in on a few things. Give me thirty minutes and then we can eat." When he notices me biting my lip, he kneels down. "Are you all right? You want me to kick Barney's ass? I can take you home if you're uncomfortable."

Beside me, Phoebe sighs. "Isn't he romantic? Let him kick Barney's ass."

My lips purse and I admonish her, "Violence is not the answer."

Suzie giggles. "You got the mom voice. You're in trouble."

If there are words every mom has learned to ignore, they're 'you're in trouble'. "Are they always like this?" I ask Max.

"You're part of our family now, and this is how our family acts."

Darn it. Those words make all kinds of butterflies take action in my stomach. They're swooning and flying and swooping like a five-year-old who just learned to do a cartwheel. Stupid butterflies. I thought they abandoned me after I married my ex and learned romance is something you read about in books, not experience.

I straighten and steel myself for whatever happens next. "Go. Do your thing. But you will be making it up to me later."

He winks. "Happy to." He stands and struts away. Yikes. I think I just poked the bear.

Phoebe watches him leave. "Who knew Pops was a romantic at heart?"

"My dad is not only romantic, he's hot."

Suzie fans her face. "The man is fifty degrees of hot. There's a reason the silver fox has women chasing him all the time."

Women chasing him all the time? Why is he after me, then? I'm a single mom trying to keep my head above water while making sure my kid doesn't get himself into more trouble.

Hailey pats my arm. "Don't let them get to you. My dad never looked at another woman twice until you walked in here all shy and asking for a job. I'm surprised it's taken him this long to make his move."

"Yeah," Suzie agrees. "I didn't figure Pops for a patient guy." Before I have a chance to have another freak-out, Suzie teases Phoebe, "I'm surprised you didn't ask him how big his meat rocket is."

Phoebe groans and hides her hands in her face. "Please don't use the words Pops and meat rocket in the same sentence."

Suzie is undeterred. "Why? You wanted to know how big everyone's meat rockets were at your bachelorette party."

Ryker growls as he walks over. "What's this about you and talking about other men's cocks?"

At the word cock, my face goes up in flames. Was I seriously excited to be included in this family five minutes ago? I was wrong.

Hailey bumps my shoulder. "Here's the thing about family – as much as they love you, they also love to embarrass you."

"Can we stop talking about family and someone answer my question about what happened at the bachelorette party?" Ryker demands.

"Don't worry, mountain man. Nothing happened. There was only one naked guy." Suzie lifts her index finger. "One."

Hailey moans. "Oh boy. Wrong thing to say."

"You let my future wife see a naked man?" Ryker points at Hailey. "You promised nothing would happen."

Ryker barely gets the words out before Aiden arrives and wraps his hand around his throat. "Best man or not, I'll kick your ass if you ever talk to Hailey with that tone of voice again." Apparently, being a detective and enforcing the law mean nothing when your wife is involved.

I force myself to my feet. Time to step in and handle this. I push my way between Ryker and Aiden. "No one is kicking anyone else's ass." I push on Ryker's chest. "You, go comfort your fiancé who is currently fifty shades of embarrassed." I point at Aiden. "And you, go sit with your wife before she opens her mouth and causes more trouble."

"Whoa! Hold on!" Suzie raises her hand. "I think there's some confusion here. I'm the troublemaker, not Hailey."

Grayson picks her up and sits back down with her in his lap. "You sure are, Munchkin."

Hailey flails her hands to shush everyone. She points to the bar where Wally, Sid, Lenny, and Barney are creeping close. "It's time."

"Boss," one of the bartenders calls to Max. "This drawer's stuck. Can you open it for me?"

Max doesn't hesitate to walk to the drawer. I notice the other bartender back up until he's nearly in the kitchen. Uh oh. Max yanks on the drawer hard, and the entire thing flies out of the cabinet. I hear a bang before glitter falls from the ceiling all over him.

His buddies laugh and slap each other on the back. Wally steps closer. "It's your own fault for scaring me with the clown."

Max folds his arms over his chest. "I don't give a shit you poured glitter all over me, but I do give a shit you just made Faith's job tomorrow ten times harder."

Wally ducks his head, and I hear him mutter a few curse words. He straightens and looks over at me. "Sorry, kid," he says and then stomps away to find a mop.

"You do realize they're going to make more of a mess than they're going to help," Hailey says as we watch Sid, Lenny, and Barney try to gather the mounds of glitter with their bare hands.

"I know, but this is how you teach children there are consequences to their actions." I lean forward and whisper, "Besides, they're going to have glitter everywhere. And I do mean everywhere."

"It's diabolical mom. This is my favorite one," Suzie declares and holds her hand up for a high-five.

I oblige because apparently when I'm around these ladies I turn into a teenager.

Max walks over and holds out his hand to me. "Time for dinner, sweetheart."

I don't hesitate to take his hand, which is another reason this whole thing with Max is freaking me out. He makes me feel entirely too comfortable and safe. I was right. He should totally come with a warning label.

Chapter 15

Interviewer: Tell me about a time you dealt with a difficult situation. Mom: I once had a four-year-old. Interviewer: You're hired.

I HESITATE BEFORE KNOCKING on the door of the offices of *We Cheat, You Eat* the next day. Do I really need to be here? While I was tossing and turning in my bed last night, I convinced myself I should talk to Hailey about me dating her dad. I don't know why. Hailey seems pretty cool with the idea. Hell, she tried to play matchmaker to us not too long ago. I should probably go home.

"Are you going to stand out there all day or come in, Faith?" Suzie shouts from the other side of the door.

I open the door and stick my head inside. "How did you know it was me?"

She points to a monitor on her desk. "Security camera."

"Security camera?" No one ever told me about a security camera when I was filling in for Suzie.

"We installed it when Phoebe was having her troubles," Suzie explains. "We hardly use it now. I switched it on when I noticed the shadow in front of the door." She shrugs. "You were standing there for like five minutes."

"And Suzie is not known for her patience," Hailey adds as she walks out of her office.

Phoebe comes running out of hers, too. "What's going on? Are we having a meeting?"

"We are not having a meeting. I came to talk to Hailey."

Hailey opens her arms wide. "Whatever you have to say to me, you can say to my posse."

"We're a posse now?" Suzie rubs her hands together, and her eyes sparkle in a way this mom interprets to mean she's up to no good. "Does this mean we get to wear matching clothes? Maybe we can get matching haircuts?"

Phoebe pales. "If you think I'm coloring my hair, you have lost your mind."

"Yes!" Suzie sticks her arm in the air in victory. "You didn't say no to matching clothes."

Phoebe buries her face in her hands. "Someone get me off the Suzie rollercoaster."

I clear my throat. "Are you sure you don't want to talk alone, Hailey? It's a delicate matter."

Her eyes widen and she claps. "You're pregnant! I'm getting a brother or sister." She yanks Suzie from her chair, and they do some weird dance. It looks like the chicken dance crossed with the robot. Hailey comes to a halt and slaps her palm to her forehead. "I'm an idiot. I'm already getting a brother of course. Ollie. But I would love a little baby brother or sister. Wink. Wink. Nudge. Nudge."

"If you want a baby around, you're going to have to make one yourself, crazy woman. My baby-making factory is closed for business." I'm forty-five for gosh sakes. I'm not ready to return to dirty diapers and staying up all night trying to coax a crying baby back to sleep. Not to mention, Max and I haven't even had sex yet.

Hailey slumps into a chair. "Then, you're not here to tell me you're pregnant?"

Suzie huffs. "We already discussed this. I'm the crazy one of the group," she tells me.

"Can't we both be crazy?"

"No," Phoebe yells. "I can't deal with two crazy friends."

"How's the wedding preparation going?" I ask her to move the talk away from babies. I'm not having a baby with Max. Geesh.

"We have the final dress fitting this week." She squeezes my hands. "You should come."

I rear back. "Um, no. The dress fitting is for close friends."

She rolls her eyes. "What do you think you are? You're the girlfriend of the man walking me down the aisle. I think you fit into the definition of close friends."

"Pay up." Hailey holds her palm out to Suzie. "I told you she picked Pops."

"But Wally's the one who rescued her in the hotel room," Suzie pouts as she digs around in her purse. She pulls out a twenty and slaps it in Hailey's palm.

Phoebe squeezes my hand again to gain my attention. "You'll come then?"

Um, I'm still stuck on her use of the word girlfriend in relation to me and Max. We've been on one date. I'm pretty sure the term girlfriend is premature.

"Come on." Hailey takes a seat next to us. "My dad doesn't introduce any of his 'women' to his friends. You know this is serious."

Women? What women? I thought he didn't date.

"You're freaking her out." Suzie points to my face, which is probably white since it feels numb. "She didn't mean friends. She meant hook-ups, but she thought the word hook-up would freak you out."

Hook-ups? How many women has he hooked up with? I don't have much experience with sex. Like embarrassing little experience. This is a disaster waiting to happen.

Hailey pats my hand. "It's like riding a bike."

"With the right man, you don't need to worry about experience. They'll take care of you," Suzie adds.

"Blech. Can we stop talking about Pops having sex?" Phoebe feigns gagging before she clears her throat and goes for the jugular. "But for the record, they're right. Don't worry and let him handle everything."

I am done with this conversation. I came here to talk to Hailey about dating her dad and she's giving me sex advice. I think she's good. I stand. "I need to go."

Hailey stops me. "But what did you come here to talk to me about?"

"Nothing. It's fine."

She laughs. "It's fine? Now I know something's up." She stands. "Come on. We can talk in my office. They'll both eavesdrop, but I think you'll be more comfortable without them right there in front of your face."

She tugs my hand and I follow her into her office. She shuts the door, and I can hear Phoebe and Suzie place their ears against it.

"You weren't kidding about the eavesdropping."

"She wasn't," Suzie shouts from the other side of the door.

I collapse in a chair and one of the dogs – I don't know if it's Lola or Leroy – whines and pads over to place its head in my lap. It looks up at me with big chocolate eyes and I'm a goner. Good thing my son isn't here to see me melt about a dog. We'd be at the shelter picking one out before I could blink.

"What's up?"

I take my time putting my thoughts in order as I run my hands through the dog's hair. "I came here to make sure you don't have a problem with me dating your dad. I'm guessing by what happened out there, you're fine with it."

She beams at me. "I'm glad my dad has finally found love."

I choke on air. "Love? It's a bit early for declarations of love."

She shrugs. "Whatever. Anything else?"

It's tempting to let things go and walk away, but I can't. I came here for a reason, after all. "I want you to know I'm not trying to replace your mom."

"Good," Suzie yells. "Her mom was horrible."

Hailey wrinkles her nose. "She kind of was. I used to idolize her after she left, but after Pops told me the whole truth of why she left, I had to face facts. She was not the mom I remembered."

"About damn time you realized the truth."

"Sorry about the cheap seats," Hailey apologizes for Suzie's behavior.

"It's fine. I'm glad you have such good friends who stick up for you and have your back."

"If you don't want her for your mom, I'll take her."

"You have a mom," Hailey yells at Suzie.

I stand and walk to the door. "You might as well come in if you're going to shout through the door anyway."

"I second Suzie. Are you open to adopting an adult child?" Phoebe bats her eyelashes.

My heart warms, and I feel tears well in my eyes. I sniff and deflect. "Do you guys ever actually get any work done?"

"Speaking of work," Hailey begins. "I've got an offer for you."

"Yeah." Suzie bobs her head. "An offer you can't refuse."

"It's an offer you don't want to refuse, not an offer you can't refuse. Can't refuse makes you sound like a mobster," Phoebe points out.

Suzie flexes her tiny bicep. "I could be a mobster."

"Anyway," Hailey says, and I return my attention to her. "Suzie can't handle being our office manager and running her brewery anymore."

"Yeah, my *husband* is a marketing genius and now I'm selling beer like crazy. Which reminds me, I have an appointment in an hour to view a space for the brewery."

"Congratulations," I tell her. "But what does this have to do with me?"

Suzie stands next to Hailey. "We'd like to offer you the position of office manager."

"You'd be a salaried employee and there are benefits," Hailey adds.

"But you do have to do some work for Ryker."

"And sometimes you need to walk the dogs." Suzie points to the dogs cuddled up in the corner ignoring our existence.

I hold up my hand. "Whoa! Hang on." I take a deep breath before diving in. "I appreciate the offer, but I'm going to pass. I'm happy to fill in when necessary, but I'm not looking for a new position."

"Is this because of what happened in Saint Louis?" Hailey asks, and I gasp.

"You know?"

Oh no, oh no. This can't be happening. If they know, then everyone knows, which means word about where I am will get out. I can't allow word to get out. I can't allow Ollie to be in danger. Dang it. Every time things start looking up, everything blows up in my face. I don't want to move. I don't want to leave Max. Wait. Erase those thoughts. Max is not a consideration. I am not tied to him.

"No, I don't know what happened, but I heard Aiden on the phone with Pops. I'm hoping you'll fill us in," she says, and I blow a breath out in relief until I realize what Max talking to Aiden means.

"Do all your partners know?" I look around at the group.

Phoebe wrinkles her nose. "I think so. I overheard Ryker talking to Pops, but he wouldn't tell me what the call was about. Trust me. I tried everything to change his mind."

Suzie raises her hand. "Grayson doesn't know anything."

Hailey snorts. "Because he can't keep a secret from you, and you can't keep a secret period."

She shrugs. "True."

Hailey grasps my hands. "It's not a big deal. You don't have to tell us. I'm sorry I brought it up."

I feel bad for lying to them, but withholding the truth isn't quite lying. "I can't tell you. Sorry." I notice the clock on the wall. "I need to go. I need to pick Ollie up from his debate team practice." I nearly make it out of the office before anyone speaks.

"Don't forget the dress fitting. It's Thursday," Phoebe says before I can escape. I lift my hand up and wave. I don't bother telling her I won't be there. I'm a mom. I know how to pick my battles.

Chapter 16

Having a kid is like watching a miniature version
of yourself gradually become cooler while you
become progressively less cool.

Max takes the cloth from my hand before leading me to a
table.

"What's wrong?" he asks once I'm sitting in a chair with him
across from me.

"What do you mean – what's wrong? What makes you think
something's wrong?"

He raises an eyebrow, and I squirm. "Sweetheart, you've been
cleaning the same spot on the pool table for fifteen minutes now.
You practically rubbed a hole into the apron. And you didn't
respond when I called your name."

Pfff. I have a feeling I'm never going to get anything past
this man. "Phoebe invited me to go wedding dress shopping
with her and the girls tomorrow. Although, it's not exactly dress
shopping since she's already picked out the dress."

He scratches his beard. "I'm not seeing what the problem is."

"It's not a problem exactly." I fiddle with the corner of the
table. "It's just…" Ugh! I don't want to admit what I'm thinking

to him, but I've known Max long enough to know he won't give up until I'm confessing. "I miss my friends. I miss my life in Saint Louis." Although, except for Valerie, my friends never felt much like family back home. I'm missing something I never had. Apparently, it's a sentimental day today.

Max lifts me out of my seat and wraps his arms around me. "I'm sorry, sweetheart. I know it must be difficult to not be able to contact your friends and family."

His arms feel entirely too good around me. I want to stay cocooned in the safety of his warmth forever, which scares the pants off of me. I do the adult thing – I lash out instead of taking comfort. "How would you know what it's like? I've been cut off from my life completely."

Max lays a hand on my cheek. "I've been there, sweetheart. When I was in Iraq, there were times I couldn't call home for weeks. It's tough."

I bury my face in his shoulder. "I'm a bitch." I'm whining about my situation when I'm safe, not in the middle of a freaking warzone.

He sways me from side to side. "You are not a bitch. You're having a moment is all."

"Stop being nice! It's making me feel worse."

I can feel his body shake with laughter. "How's this? Get your pretty ass back to work!"

I bend backwards to look at him. "You didn't use the barky voice. And you have a big smile on your face."

"I find it hard to yell at you. This does not bode well for my future."

I wink. "But it does for mine."

His eyes warm before his head dips and his lips find mine. I rise on my toes and thread my fingers through his hair. He groans and the sound reverberates on my lips. I gasp and his tongue sneaks inside my mouth. He doesn't plunder. He gently explores my mouth as his hands rove across my back. This is his way of offering me comfort and I'm happy to accept his offer.

When he ends the kiss, I'm sure I look starstruck.

"Feeling better?" he asks between pants for breath. I nod. "Good." He takes a step back and smacks my ass before walking off whistling a tune.

I fan myself. How is it possible for a kiss to turn my legs into jelly?

♥♥♥

"You're here!" Phoebe cries and rushes toward me when I walk into the bridal boutique the next day because I totally caved and decided to join her for the dress fitting. I didn't have much choice after my talk with Max, and the phone and text assault from Phoebe, Hailey, and Suzie.

Phoebe throws her arms around me and jumps up and down. I pat her back.

"How much have you had to drink?"

She giggles. "Only two glasses of champagne," she says in a voice entirely too loud for the fancy boutique.

I step out of her embrace. "How can I help?"

She takes my hand and drags me to the rear of the store where Hailey and Suzie are sitting on a sofa sipping champagne.

"Mom's here. Act normal," Suzie says when she notices us.

Hailey snorts. "As if your mom is normal." She's not lying. Suzie's mom is crazy with a capital C. She actually tried to give Ollie the sex talk when we met her at Suzie's wedding party. Ollie's fifteen, I already embarrassed my way through the sex talk with him.

Suzie pats the sofa next to her. "Come. Sit. We have champagne."

I take a seat but refuse the champagne. "I'm driving and I have a kid at home."

"What's having a kid have to do with drinking?" Hailey asks.

"I'm a single mom. Whenever I have more than one glass of wine, my kid falls and breaks a bone. Trust me. No parent wants to be in the emergency room smelling like wine with a kid with a broken bone." The bachelorette party notwithstanding, I usually stick to one glass of wine.

"You can't tell me some stupid doctor or nurse accused you of abuse. You'll like Supermom." Suzie looks like she's ready to march off and give someone a piece of her mind.

I pat her arm. "The nurse was a single mom, too, and we single moms stick together."

"Are you guys ready?" Phoebe shouts from the other side of a curtain.

"Bring it," Suzie shouts back.

Phoebe walks into the room, and I gasp. Her wedding gown is the most beautiful thing I've ever seen. It's classic and romantic. And yet it's sexy with the v-neckline combined with double beaded spaghetti straps extending to the low cut back. There are sequined lace appliques to give the gown a soft and subtle sparkle. To top it all off, there's a lace train.

"What do you think?"

I stand. "What do I think? I think you're stunning."

"I think Ryker's going to want to rip the gown off of you before you make it down the aisle," Hailey adds.

"And I think I was right to push you into making this wedding happen." Suzie raises her arm in victory.

Phoebe grasps my hands. "Now, it's your turn."

"My turn? What are you talking about? I'm not getting married."

An image of Max in a tuxedo waiting for me at the alter pops into my head. I bet the man looks absolutely scrumptious in a tux. I slap myself upside the head. What am I thinking? We've been on exactly one date and I'm having wedding daydreams! This is why I should have stayed away from the man. It would be way too easy to fall in love with him.

"No, but you will be at my wedding."

I'm planning on wearing one of my tried-and-true dresses. One good thing about not being in Saint Louis. No one in this city has seen any of the three dresses I managed to bring with me when we packed up our lives and ran.

"I'm buying you a dress and that's all there is to it." Phoebe tugs me toward the dressing rooms.

I dig my feet in. "I can't let you buy me a dress."

"It's not like she doesn't have the money," Suzie says from her place on the sofa where she's now kneeling while bouncing up and down like she's a toddler.

I frown at her. "Sit on the sofa properly or stand."

She immediately stands. "Sorry."

Hailey laughs and raises her hand for a high-five. I stare at her hand for a few seconds before slapping it with mine.

"Please." Phoebe flutters her eyelashes at me. "Please, let me buy you a dress as a thank you for your help with the wedding."

"I didn't do much."

Hailey snorts. "Seriously? Do you know how many times I had to hear her bitch about the flowers? And then you come in and – bam! – within five minutes the flowers are chosen, and the colors are picked."

Phoebe tugs me to the dressing room. "At least look at the dresses I picked out for you."

I gasp when I see the navy-blue chiffon cocktail dress hanging there. I reach out to touch it before snatching my hand back. I can't do this. I can't accept such a generous gift. Phoebe pushes me into the room.

"Go on. Try it. You know you want to."

I can try it on without her buying it for me, can't I? I slide the curtain to the dressing area closed and strip off my sweater and jeans. Phoebe pokes her head in. I scream and try to cover my body, although I'm not completely naked since I'm wearing a bra and panties.

Phoebe's eyes sweep over my body. "Oh, honey. We need to go lingerie shopping."

I look down at what I'm wearing. I'm in a white utility bra I bought in a three-pack at some discount store and a pair of granny pants I'm not sure where I got.

Suzie peeks her head into the dressing room. "Sorry, Mamma, but this is not going to fly. I'll even go to a lingerie store to deal with this disaster."

"Geez. Why don't we invite the entire store in here to comment on my underwear choices?"

"It's only me out here, and I do not need to see your underwear," Hailey comments. "But if Suzie thinks you need new underwear, you need new underwear."

"I got this," Phoebe says and rushes off still in her wedding gown.

"Do you think she realizes she's still in her wedding gown?" I ask the room.

Suzie rolls her eyes. "She'd probably wear it every day from now until the wedding if we let her."

"At least she'd get some use out of it." I sound bitter because I might be the teeniest bit annoyed about spending hundreds of dollars on a dress I wore once to marry an asshole.

Phoebe rushes back carrying a pile of lacy things. "Oh good," she says when she sees me. "You haven't tried the dress on yet. Try this bra and panties on with the dress."

She shoves the lingerie into my arms and then slides the curtain closed. "And don't look at how much it costs."

Of course, now I have to look at the price. She's out of her mind. Two hundred dollars for a scrap of silk! She's lost it. But I'm dying to see what the silk feels like against my skin. I strip and put on the panties she picked out. Wow. I feel sexy.

Hailey sticks her head in, and I squeal. "What is it with you women? Haven't you heard of privacy?"

"It's not like I haven't seen what you've got." She looks me up and down and whistles. "Pops is going to lose his mind when he sees you in those."

"I swear you say those things because you know they freak me out," Phoebe grumbles.

Hailey winks and mouths *I totally do.*

Since Hailey doesn't look like she has any plans to move anytime soon, I shimmy into the dress while she watches. "Gorgeous."

"Let me see." Suzie pushes Hailey out of the way. "Yep. This is the dress."

"Great. We can pay and get out of here. I'm starving," Hailey announces.

Suzie rolls her eyes. "You're always starving."

"I need to get home to Ollie."

"We'll pick up a pizza on our way to your place," Suzie says like it's a foregone conclusion they're joining me at my apartment.

Hailey throws an arm around my shoulders. "We can leave you alone if you like."

My mouth automatically opens to tell her I'll be fine on my own, but those words don't come out. Instead, I find myself saying, "Nah. It'll be a nice change for Ollie."

Chapter 17

A hamburger walks into a bar. The bartender says, "We don't serve food!" The hamburger says "That's okay. I want a drink." ~ Text from Pops to Hailey

POPS

It's Monday evening, and I'm feeling restless. I didn't see Faith all weekend since she's feeling guilty about spending last weekend with me. I missed her. And, if I'm being honest with myself, I missed the kid too. I miss having a kid around. I'm too young to be a grandfather, but I'm ready for Hailey to give me some grandchildren all the same.

Since the crowds on Monday are all but non-existent, there's no need for a bartender, which means I'm standing behind the bar twiddling my thumbs as my buddies play poker in the corner. I fiddle around on my phone to pass the time. Social media is for conspiracy theorists, but I finally succumbed to the never-ending badgering from Hailey and made a Twitter and Facebook account for McGraw's Pub.

I open the Twitter app and click on the notification button. What the hell? Why do I have over one hundred notifications?

I read the first notification – *proud of you!* Proud of me? For what? I switch over to the pub's home page and read the last tweet. *It's time for me to come out of the closet.*

I throw the phone on the bar and stomp to the poker playing asses.

"Took you long enough." Wally smirks.

"Jokes about sexual orientation are not funny."

Lenny's head whips up, and he snarls at Wally. "You made a joke about his sexual orientation?"

Lenny is bi-sexual. When we were stuck in some backwater rat hole in the middle of the desert for days and everyone was bragging about their conquests, he accidentally confessed to a male conquest. It didn't take us long to figure out he doesn't have a preference for men or women. After we said we accepted him anyway – you don't kick a brother who has your back during an armed conflict out of the brotherhood without good reason – he told us the discussion was closed. We've tiptoed around the subject ever since.

"Ah, fuck." Wally wipes a hand down his face. "I didn't think. I'm sorry." He removes his phone from his pocket. "I'll have the tweet and any trace of it removed asap."

"Even I know better than to make those kinds of offending jokes." Barney purses his lips and shakes his head. Of course, he ruins his whole innocent act a second later when he opens his mouth again. "Moving on. How long do you think it will be before Pops and Faith do the horizontal mambo? I've got twenty bucks on six months."

"No way. Have you seen Pops?" Lenny's eyes travel over my body as he checks me out. When he licks his lips, I smack him upside the head.

"Knock it off," I order him and then fist the back of Barney's t-shirt and haul him out of the booth. "And you. Enough with the bets and disrespecting Faith." I shake him to get my point across.

"He disrespected Ma?" At Ollie's question, I force myself to release Barney. Faith would skin me alive if I was violent in front of her kid.

"What's up, son?"

Ollie ignores me to step right up in Barney's space. "Did you disrespect my mother?" He's several inches shorter and about a foot narrower than Barney but he doesn't back down.

I take a hold of his t-shirt and tug him back. He fights me the whole way.

"Let me go." I lift him off the floor and his arms flail. "I need to teach him a lesson."

I bend down to get in his face. "And what does your mom think of violence?"

"She says it's not the answer. But she also says you have to stick up for yourself and those who are weaker than you."

Of course, she does. The woman also claims not to know where her son gets his savior complex from. I can tell her – from her.

Wally and the rest of the gang get to their feet. They leave Barney all on his own to stand behind Ollie. "We got your back, kid," Wally insists. Sid and Lenny grunt in agreement.

"I was only having fun," Barney whines.

I open my mouth to explain how it's only fun if no one gets hurt, but Ollie gets there before me. "It's not okay to have fun at someone else's expense. Not ever."

This kid. My heart swells with pride. I know I have no right to feel proud of him. He's not my kid, but I do anyway. I place a hand on his shoulder and squeeze.

"Does your mom know you're here?"

He blushes but refuses to look away. "No, she thinks I'm at debate practice."

I raise an eyebrow. "Lying to your mom?"

He straightens his back. "A necessary evil. I need to talk to you." He looks around at the men gathered near us. "In private."

I gotta give it to him, this kid has balls.

"Sure." I point toward my office. "You want a coke?"

He shakes his head. "Ma doesn't allow soda during the week."

Damn. This kid is perfect.

We walk to my office, and I take a seat behind my desk while Ollie paces in front of me. I relax and wait him out. I've got time. It's not like there's a crowd of people demanding drinks. Besides, my brothers will let me know if there's a problem on the floor.

"How can I help you?" I ask when a few minutes have passed without him speaking.

He takes a deep breath and blows it out before answering. "I need to talk to you about you dating my mom."

Those were the last words I expected him to say. "Is my dating your mom a problem?"

"I don't want her to get hurt. My dad hurt her enough to last a lifetime."

Good to know. I assumed by the menace rolling off of her anytime her ex was mentioned, she didn't love him anymore, but it's good to have confirmation her ex won't be a problem.

"I can't promise to never hurt her." His jaw clenches, and I raise a hand for him to hold up and allow me to explain. "I'm a man. I'm going to make mistakes that piss her off … er … make her angry. But I promise I will never hurt her intentionally."

"Good." He nods. "Mom needs more happiness in her life. But she's not the kind of girl you have fun with, you hear me?"

I tilt my chair forward. "How do you know about girls you only have fun with?"

Do I need to have the sex talk with him? My sex talk is rusty, but I bet giving it to a boy will be a hell of a lot easier than giving it to my daughter was. I still cringe when I think of my floundering attempt at a sex talk with Hailey. Sock puppets was really not the way to go.

Ollie rolls his eyes. "I'm fifteen. Not some loser freshman."

I smile. Those were the days. Being in high school and thinking you knew everything. If only.

"What are your intentions with my mom?"

My smile drops. This kid doesn't pull any punches. "I am serious about your mom."

"I'm not saying I'm ready for you to be my stepdad but good."

Stepdad. My heart skips at the word. I'd love to be Ollie's stepdad. Not that he needs one. Faith is doing a great job raising him to be a man all by herself, but I'd love to lift some of her burdens. I raised Hailey almost entirely on my own. I know how tough and lonely it can get.

"Do you give this talk to all of your mom's suitors?" I might as well pry while I've got the kid talking.

"Nah. You're the first man she's dated since Silas left."

Possessive feelings stir in my stomach, but the last thing Ollie needs to see is me getting all possessive over his mom.

"You always call your dad Silas?"

He looks down at the carpet. "Only when Mom's not around. She thinks I should call him Dad. I don't know why. It's not like he ever acted like a dad. I haven't seen him in years. A dad doesn't abandon his kid."

"I won't tell her, but in front of me, feel free to call him whatever you want."

He grins. "Ass?"

"Language. Your mom will have my ass if you come home using those kinds of words."

His grin changes into a smirk. "She doesn't know I'm here."

I stand. "Speaking of which. Let me give you a ride back to school."

"Thanks."

"And you will be telling your mom you came to the pub today."

"You're as bad as Ma," he whines.

I raise an eyebrow. "Why are you telling your mom about coming here today?"

"Because lying to Ma is bad."

"And?"

"And sneaking off from a school event is wrong."

I clap him on the shoulder. "Good. Now, let's go. Maybe I can get you back before your mom shows up and freaks out when she finds you gone."

Chapter 18

My mother's love is unconditional. My temper on
the other hand ....

"Ma." Ollie squirms as I straighten his tie. "I don't know why
I have to wear a tie."

"Because," I explain for the millionth time, "it's a wedding.
We dress up for events like weddings. Would you rather stay
home?" His eyes light up, and I remind him, "Lenny, Barney,
Sid, and Wally will be there. Not to mention Hailey and Aiden
and Suzie and Grayson."

I don't mention Max. His obvious dislike of my boss has
waned, but I'm not sure how he feels about me dating in
general. Max isn't the first man I've dated since my divorce, but
it's the first man Ollie has known about. I went out on a few
blind dates when Valerie refused to take no for an answer, but
Ollie doesn't know about any of them seeing as they were all
certified failures.

"Do you think I can sit with Hailey during the ceremony?"

"Sorry, kiddo. Hailey's the maid of honor, but I'm sure Lenny,
Barney, Sid, and Wally will let us sit with them."

"What about Max?"

"What about him?" I go for nonchalant.

"Can I sit with him? After all, you're dating."

I glance at the clock. Do we have time for a talk before we leave? Not really. But I don't have much of a choice. "Let's have a seat."

"No. Not another talk," Ollie whines.

I ignore the whining and dive right in. "How do you feel about me dating Max?"

"I'm fine with it," he says with a little cough at the end, which tells me he's lying.

There's no time for subtle. Our ride will be here any second now. "Why are you lying?"

"I'm not lying! I don't have a problem with Max."

I narrow my eyes and study him. He may not be exactly lying, but he's definitely not telling the whole truth either. My phone dings to alert me our car has arrived. "Don't think we won't talk about this later, mister."

"You look pretty, Ma."

I snort. "Nice try, kid. Nice try."

When we arrive at the church, most of the guests are already seated. But since the preacher isn't here yet, I'm calling it a win. Max sees us enter and doesn't hesitate to walk right on over to us. The subtle shake of my head and my eyes widening mean nothing to him.

"Hi, Spitfire," he says and kisses my cheek.

I narrow my eyes on him. We shouldn't be kissing in front of Ollie! I've barely had the talk with him about me dating. A talk during which it became clear he's hiding things from me.

I need to ferret out the truth before we start indulging in public displays of affection.

"Gross." Ollie gags. "I see Wally. See you there, Ma." He takes off without a backward glance.

I debate following him, but Max tags my hand. "Let him go. He's safe here."

I take a deep breath and let all the tension about how my son will handle my dating go. It's Phoebe's day. She doesn't deserve to have a deranged single mother going all *Die Hard* during her wedding.

I change the subject instead. "How did the guys react when Phoebe finally told them she picked you to walk her down the aisle?"

Max doesn't answer my question. Instead, he drags me near, and his lips meet mine for a kiss you can probably get smote for when in a church and not legally wed. When he lifts his head, I'm clutching his lapels and my heart is thumping out of control. Those stupid butterflies are doing acrobatics in my stomach. I place a hand on my middle and use the mom voice to tell them to calm down. They ignore me.

"Hi, sweetheart," Max whispers.

Before my mind manages to form words, there's a commotion in the vestibule as Hailey and Suzie walk out of the bride's room. Oh wow. They look gorgeous. They're wearing floor-length navy-blue bridesmaid dresses with spaghetti straps and ruched chiffon bodices. I look down at my own navy-blue dress. Did Phoebe intend for me to match the bridal party?

I realize the music inside the church has changed in preparation of the wedding party procession. "Oh shoot. I better find a seat. I'll see you afterwards."

Max doesn't let me go. He grasps my hand and leads me to an usher. "Seat her in the first pew, please."

I gasp. "What are you doing?" I hiss. "I'm not family."

"Sweetheart," is the only thing he says.

"Saying sweetheart is not an answer!" The usher offers me his arm, but I refuse to take it.

"Phoebe," Suzie yells. "Faith is being difficult."

My eyes widen. "Don't you dare bring the bride out here. The doors are open. Everyone will see her."

Suzie shrugs. "Then, you'll have to walk down the aisle with the usher, won't you?"

Grayson pushes her out of the way. "Enough, troublemaker. I got this." He whistles and motions to Ryker who's standing at the alter waiting for his bride.

The next thing I know Ryker is prowling down the aisle, his eyes focused on me. I raise my hands and step back, but Max is there preventing my escape.

Ryker arrives and takes my hand. "Faith."

I shake my head. "I can't. I'm not Phoebe's mom."

"Thank god!" Suzie says, and Grayson shushes her.

Ryker bends down and whispers to me, "Phoebe's mom was not a good person, but you are. I honestly don't think we'd be here today if it weren't for you."

"I didn't—"

He places his finger on my mouth. "No, I don't want to hear your denials. And don't tell me you didn't have anything to do with her finally agreeing to talk about having children. She cherishes your friendship and asked me to make sure you sit in the front row with the rest of her family. We good?"

What can I say? I'm holding up the entire wedding ceremony. "I g-g-guess."

He holds out his elbow and escorts me down the aisle to the first pew where Ollie is waiting with Max's friends. He kisses the top of my head before returning to his place at the altar. I sniff. I didn't realize Phoebe considered me family. Let alone wanted me to sit in the first pew with the rest of her family.

"You're not going to cry are you, Ma?" Ollie whispers in a voice loud enough for the entire church to hear.

"Lesson about women," Wally says. "If they want to cry, you let them cry." He reaches around Ollie to hand me an honest to goodness handkerchief.

The music gets louder, and I turn to watch Suzie and Grayson walk down the aisle. Despite his firm grip on her arm, she still manages to trip. He catches her before she falls on her face and drags her the rest of the way down the aisle. Hailey and Aiden are up next. Once they are at their places, the music changes, and everyone stands.

The doors open, and I hear gasps as Phoebe comes into view. I don't look her way. I've seen her dress. I watch Ryker instead. His hands fist and he takes one step forward. But then he shakes his head and steps back.

"Pay up, sucker," Sid says.

Barney slaps a bill into his palm. "I was sure he'd pull an Aiden and rush down the aisle to meet her."

Ollie leans close to me to whisper, "These guys bet about everything."

"And what do we think about gambling?"

"Not every comment I make is a chance for a teaching moment," he mumbles.

Max and Phoebe reach the alter, and I feel tears well in my eyes at the look of love Phoebe shares with Ryker. I should have known it wasn't a good sign when Silas tapped his watch during our wedding ceremony.

"Who gives this woman to be married to this man?" the preacher asks.

The group of men at my pew stand. Together with Max, they shout, "She gives herself but with our blessings."

Phoebe looks over at the men and her smile is practically blinding. "Thank you," she whispers and blows them a kiss before turning back to her almost-husband.

Max kisses her forehead and places her hand in Ryker's. "Treat her right," he orders.

Ryker isn't intimidated. He's too busy ogling his bride. "Always."

Max steps away from the couple and takes a seat next to me. He places his arm around my shoulder and pulls me near. He frowns when he notices the handkerchief I'm clasping in my hands. He yanks it away and throws it at Wally. Then, he replaces it with one of his own.

"Caveman," I whisper.

The rest of the ceremony passes quickly. Before I know it, Ryker is kissing the daylights out of his bride, and the guys are hooting and hollering. I jump to my feet and clap as the wedding party passes our pew.

"Come on." Max takes my hand and drags me out into the aisle behind them. I motion for Ollie to follow us. "He's fine. My brothers are going to take care of him today."

I bristle. "I'm perfectly capable of taking care of my own son."

"Sure you are, but when was the last time someone offered you the chance to let loose and not worry about him?"

Good question. I can't remember the last time I had a real night off. Silas was pretty much absent from Ollie's life from the beginning. We were married, but you wouldn't be able to tell from how often my *husband* was around. Considering my ex couldn't find a job if it hit him in the forehead, he sure had a lot of places to be.

When we arrive at Max's truck, he spins me around and crowds me against the door. "What do you say? You gonna let my brothers take care of your boy and let loose for a change?"

"I say I don't trust your brothers one bit. He'll probably be smoking, drinking whisky, and losing his shirt at poker before we arrive at the reception."

"Don't worry. They play for pretzels," Max teases.

"I'm holding you responsible for the consequences, including any bail money."

"Have you met my daughter? I always have bail money ready." He winks before sealing his lips to mine. I grasp his face in my hands, but the smooth skin feels strange and I end up frowning.

Max pulls back to ask, "You don't like me cleanshaven?" Strangely enough, I don't. I shake my head. "Then, I'll never shave again."

He sounds like he'd do pretty much anything to make me happy. And doesn't that idea scare the living daylights out of me.

Chapter 19

If I ever go missing, follow my kid. He can find me no matter where I try to hide.

WHEN WE WALK INTO the hotel where the wedding reception is taking place, my mouth drops open at the vision in front of me. "Wow," is all I can say. I've never been in a hotel with marble floors, painted murals on the ceiling, and a doorman in the lobby before.

Max entwines his hand with mine and leads me to the ball-room. I look around the place, but I'm not seeing the flowers and balloons. I'm searching for Ollie.

I tug on Max's hand when he directs us to our table. "I need to speak to Ollie first."

He changes directions, and we head to the table with his brothers. As expected, they've got the cards out and are showing Ollie how to play poker. I groan. Isn't he a bit young for poker?

"Ollie," I call when we're close to the table.

"Hi, Ma," he answers without looking up from his cards.

"We need to have a word."

He waves a hand in my direction. "Behave, listen to what my elders tell me, and don't drink the adult punch. Got it."

Max chuckles until I elbow him in the gut. "Shut it." He clears his throat, but I can see the mirth lingering in his eyes.

"We need to talk," I insist.

"What about this time, Ma?"

I cross my arms over my chest. "How about why you lied to me before we left the house today?"

"I didn't lie," he says and coughs. Gotcha!

"Tell it to another mother."

"Do we have to do this now?" he whines.

"Do you want me to air all your dirty laundry in front of your new friends?"

Lenny, Wally, Sid, and Barney fold their cards on the table. "Better listen to your mom, kid," Wally says.

Ollie jumps to his feet and marches out of the room. I pray for patience before following him. Teenage temper tantrum here we come.

He stops in the hallway and whirls around to face me. "What? Do you have to embarrass me in front of everyone? I wasn't doing anything wrong!"

I let him flail about for a minute. This isn't my first rodeo. I know better than to interrupt a temper tantrum.

"Tell me what you lied about. Promise you'll behave. And then we're done here," I explain once he runs out of steam.

"I didn't lie," he says and coughs.

"Son," Max says, and I startle. I didn't realize he'd followed us into the hallway. "You need to work on your tell or my brothers are going to annihilate you in poker."

"My tell?"

"It's how your mom knows you're lying."

I elbow him. "I know he's lying because my superpower is being a mom." The last thing I need is Ollie figuring out his tell.

"Of course," Max concedes.

"Come on, Ollie. Tell me why you lied about being fine with Max and I dating." Next to me, I feel Max stiffen, but I ignore him to concentrate on my son who's blushing and looking at the carpet as if it's the most fascinating thing he's seen in his fifteen years on this earth.

"Son, did you forget to tell your mom something?"

I whirl around to face Max. "What are you talking about?"

He ignores me. "I told you if you didn't tell her, I will."

I grip his forearm and squeeze. "What happened?" My mom panic meter is inching toward the red zone.

"Ollie?"

Ollie grunts. "I went to see Pops. Are you happy now? Now, you know the big secret. Can I get back to the party now?"

He tries marching past me, but I catch his arm and stop him. "Not so fast. Why did you go see Max?"

"I wanted to make sure he was good enough for you! You deserve to be treated better than Silas treated you!"

I sniff, and he groans. "You're getting the look again." I pull him into my arms and squeeze him tight. "You're suffocating me," he complains, but he puts his arms around me and hugs me back.

"I love you, Ollie. You are the best son a mother could ask for." Tears are rolling down my cheeks now and I don't care. My kid is the absolute best in the entire world. No, the universe. Single mother – One Million. Universe – Zero. Hah! Take that!

Phoebe rushes over to us. "Is everything all right? Are you okay, Faith? What happened?"

I lift my head and loosen my arms, and Ollie takes the opportunity to escape. "Bye, Ma. I'll behave. Promise!"

"My kid is awesome!" I tell Phoebe.

Her brow wrinkles as she stares at me. "And this is why you're crying?"

Max places his arm around my shoulders. "It's a parent thing," he says. "You'll understand some day."

She looks over at her brand-new husband, and her face gets all mushy. "I hope so." She offers me a key card. "Here. You might want to…" She circles her face with a finger.

Max takes the card. "Thanks, darling. We'll be right back."

"Take your time," she says as Max hauls me away.

The second we're in the room Max whirls around and slams his lips down on mine before the door even closes. I gasp, and his tongue pushes inside. His hands spear into my hair, and he tilts my head to dive deep into my mouth.

I spread my hands on his chest. He can't possibly be in his fifties. No one in their fifties has muscle definition like this unless they're a rock star. I can feel the heat emanating from his skin as I pet him and suddenly touching his bare skin is the most important thing in the world. I push his tuxedo jacket off his shoulders. He releases my hair to let the jacket fall to the floor, and I attack the pearl buttons of his shirt.

Max chuckles. "In a hurry?"

"In case you forgot, we have a wedding reception to attend." I sound desperate, and I don't care. I can't remember when the last time I had sex was, and my body is warning me it's going to go up in flames if I don't rectify the omission immediately.

"In that case…" He smirks and unbuttons his shirt to reveal a chest worthy of the front cover of *Sports Illustrated*.

"Holy cow." My hands reach out to trace his pectoral muscles. His nipples tighten, and he moans before snatching my hands away. I mewl in protest. "I want to touch you." I look down at the prominent bulge in his pants and lick my lips.

He groans. "You're killing me." He bends down and – whoosh! – suddenly I'm in the air. He walks to the bed, which is covered in rose petals.

I giggle. "We can't. Not on their marriage bed."

He rotates in a circle until he finds what he's looking for. In a corner in front of the fireplace is a chaise lounge. He lays me down on the lounge before sinking to his knees in front of me.

I try to touch him, but he's too far away. "Come closer."

He takes my hands and holds them above my head. "Sorry, sweetheart. If you touch me, I won't be able to control myself. And we don't have time for me to worship you the way you deserve to be worshiped."

I stick my bottom lip out. "I don't want to be worshiped. I want to have sex."

"Don't worry. I'll take care of you." He places my hands on the armrest. "Leave them there."

I normally hate when a man orders me around, but I don't hesitate to nod as I watch his hands skim along my legs and slowly travel upward. I'm not wearing pantyhose and a trail of goosebumps follows in his wake. He reaches the hem of my dress and pushes it upwards until my lace panties are revealed.

Heat flares in his eyes, and he growls. I guess he likes the panties. I owe Phoebe big time for guilt tripping me into letting her buy them for me.

His thumbs rub circles in my upper thighs as he bends forward and sniffs. "I can smell how excited you are."

My entire body flushes at his dirty words. He looks up and smirks at me. "You're even sexier when you blush. It makes me want to say all kinds of dirty things to you, but we don't have the time."

I squirm. "Maybe you should get a move on then."

He laughs, but his hands move to my panties. He drags them down my legs until they're hanging off of one foot. I'm now completely bare to the man. The lights are on, and it's the middle of the day. If he were anyone else, I'd be embarrassed to be laid out for him like a buffet. But this is Max. He makes me feel safe even now.

He takes my right leg and tosses it over his shoulder before dipping his head and diving in. He licks my seam, and I moan before throwing my left leg over the back of the lounge in order to give him better access.

"Good girl," he mutters. The words vibrate against my skin, and I squirm as my veins flood with need. He's barely touching me, and I'm ready to go off like a rocket on the fourth of July.

His mouth latches onto my clit, and he sucks until I see stars. My hands move to clasp his head to keep him right where I need him, and then I'm riding his mouth for all I'm worth. His tongue circles my clit a few times before returning to suck it.

Heat builds in my middle and I feel tingles throughout my legs. "I'm close," I gasp.

Max shoves two fingers into me and curls them causing the warmth in my belly to increase until I detonate. "Oh god, oh god," I pant.

"Say my name," he rumbles. "When you come, you say my name."

I tilt my head forward to look into his eyes and whimper, "Max." I can't hold his eyes, though, as pleasure I've never felt before courses through my body. My head falls back, and my eyes close as my back arches off the chaise. He continues to suck and thrust his fingers inside me as the pleasure slowly wanes.

"Pops," Hailey shouts before the door opens. "We need you downstairs. Your speech is coming up in the program."

I scramble to cover myself in time, but the daughter of the man who just gave me the best orgasm in my life walks in before I have a chance. Her eyes widen as she takes us in. Then, she spins around and leaves without saying a word.

"Who had sex in Phoebe's hotel room?" She yells as she walks away.

I collapse into the chaise lounge. "Tell me I imagined your daughter walking in on us."

His chest rumbles with his laughter. "Sorry, sweetheart. I can't lie to you."

My face heats as I think about walking into the ballroom with everyone knowing what we've been up to.

Max places a finger under my chin and lifts my head, so I have to look him in the eyes. "We're adults. We weren't doing a thing wrong."

"True but—"

He moves his finger to cover my mouth. "No. I'm not letting you feel embarrassed about what was one of the hottest, sexiest things to happen to me in my life."

He doesn't let me answer before he's hauling me to my feet. "Now, go clean up your face and do whatever it is you women need to do to make yourselves more beautiful. I have a speech to give."

When I don't move fast enough, he pats me on the ass.

"Fine. I'm going. I'm going."

Chapter 20

Parenting is basically whispering for fuck's sake under your breath before answering to your name.

I'M STILL FLOATING ON a cloud when Wednesday evening arrives. Max and I have enjoyed a morning coffee break together every day this week. And coffee break is totally code for making out like teenagers on the sofa in his office. He makes me feel like a teenager and not the forty-five-year-old single mom I am.

I'm keeping an eye on Ollie to make sure he doesn't have a problem with Max and I dating, but thus far he seems to be handling things fine.

"Stop staring at me, Ma," he complains.

"I'm not staring." I'm totally staring.

"I'm fine. I'm not some five-year-old boy who misses his dad. I'm fifteen. I'm practically an adult." I snort. As if a fifteen-year-old has a clue how the world works. "I can handle you dating Pops." He grimaces. "As long as you don't kiss in front of me because gross."

"How do you know I'm thinking about—" My question is cut off by the doorbell.

"Praise the lord," Ollie says before running for the door. "It's Hailey," he says before opening the door and inviting her in.

"Hey, Ollie," she says and throws her arm around his neck to give him a noogie. She's tall at five-feet-eight inches and easily towers over him.

He pushes her away. "Knock it off."

I stand between the two of them before they can get in a wrestling match on my living room floor. "Ollie, homework." I point to the kitchen table. He mumbles under his breath as he stomps off. I ignore whatever he's mumbling. Whatever it is, is not a hill worth dying on.

"What's up, Hailey?" I motion to the couch. "Have a seat."

"No time to sit. I'm only here to invite you to girls' night out tonight."

I wrinkle my brow. "But it's Wednesday."

"I finished a big case today. We're celebrating."

"Congrats!" I say automatically.

"What do you say? You want to come out with us?"

I lean close to whisper, "Isn't this weird? You saw me and your dad… you know."

She waves my concern away with a flick of her hand. "Didn't we have this conversation already? I feel like I'm having déjà vu."

"Smart ass."

She whips out a salute. "Private Smartass. Reporting for duty."

Ollie chuckles behind me. Oh god, Ollie. Did he hear? Before I can explain the anti-swearing rule again, he raises his hands in surrender. "I know. I know. No swearing."

"I don't want to leave Ollie alone. It's a school night."

Hailey bounces on her toes. "Aiden and Grayson are at my house playing some video game. They asked if Ollie can join them."

Ollie's on his feet and pleading in front of me in a blink of an eye. "Can I, Ma? Can I?"

I purse my lips. "Is your homework for tomorrow done?"

He bobs his head. "Yes. I'm working on a history paper, but it's not due until Monday." He flutters his lashes and widens his big, brown eyes. I thought I was immune to those puppy dog eyes. I guess not. I give in.

"Fine. But you need to be home before ten."

"Aiden will make sure he's home by ten." Hailey crosses her heart. "Promise."

"I guess it's all right then," I say and Ollie shouts, "Yes!"

"We'll drop him off on our way to the pub."

I've been railroaded, but Ollie is grinning wide at the chance to spend time with Hailey's husband. The poor kid is starved for adult male companionship. Ugh. Another example of how I suck as a single mother. Single Mom – Zero. Universe – One.

"Do I need to change?" I'm in a pair of jeans and long sleeve t-shirt. My outfit doesn't exactly scream night out.

"You look gorgeous as ever. Come on." She hustles us out of the apartment.

We arrive at McGraw's a little after seven. Hailey walks in first and shouts, "Honey, I'm home!"

When I follow her in, the cheering intensifies. "Told you, she'd show," Max says as he prowls toward me.

"Pay up, suckers," Wally exclaims.

"Were they betting on whether I'd show?" I ask Max. At his nod, I shake my head. "Will they bet on anything?"

"When we were in the desert, they'd bet on how many scorpions they'd see in one day. Then, they'd catch a few and race them and bet on which one would win the race." Scorpions? I shiver. No thanks.

He gives me a quick peck. "What the heck?" I exclaim when his lips leave mine way before I'm ready.

"I figured after Saturday you'd want to keep the personal displays of affection to a minimum."

I smack his chest. "Thanks for reminding me, numbskull."

"Does this mean we can tell dirty jokes in front of Faith now?" Barney asks, and Max growls.

Suzie arrives and pushes Max out of the way. "Girls' night. Men not allowed."

"You do know I own the place, Shorty?"

She waves a hand in dismissal. "I also know you don't need to be here every night. They're called staff for a reason."

Before he has a chance to respond, Suzie takes my arm and tugs me across the pub to where Hailey's sitting. Phoebe's on her honeymoon in Costa Rica. Probably laying on a beach drinking a fruity cocktail while soaking up the sun. Lucky woman.

"Thanks for coming out," Suzie says as I take my seat.

Max arrives and places a glass of wine in front of me. "Here you go, sweetheart." He kisses my head and saunters off. I watch his ass as he leaves. It is one fine ass. I've had my hands on it, but I've yet to touch the skin there. Max won't allow us to pass second base on his sofa during coffee breaks. And trust me, I've done everything I can to move things along.

"How does this work?" Suzie asks.

I take a sip of my wine because I have no clue what she's talking about. I'm not the only one.

"How does what work?" Hailey asks.

"You know." She wiggles her eyebrows. "How do we hear all the good gossip about Faith and Pops when Pops is your dad?"

I cough and spray the wine I was sipping across the table. Suzie throws me a napkin. I clean up as I ask, "Is this why I'm here? For you to pry into my relationship with your dad."

Hailey holds up her hands. "Whoa. I didn't say anything of the sort." She points to Suzie. "Crazy girl did."

"I'm glad you at least acknowledge I'm the crazy one in this relationship." She tips her non-existent hat. "Queen Crazy at your service."

"She's been watching The Crown," Hailey fills in.

I'm not seeing the connection. "I'm pretty sure Queen Elizabeth isn't crazy. A snob? Yeah, for sure. A force to be reckoned with? No doubt. A crazy person? Nah."

"Please." Suzie snorts. "You have to be crazy to put up with her family." She leans closer. "Do you think she holds onto Prince Philip's ears when she's riding his disco stick? I mean those things are huge. They're practically made to be used as handles."

Hailey rolls her eyes. "They have separate bedrooms. She probably hasn't seen his disco stick in decades. Besides, they're old. Old people and sex? Blech." Her eyes widen when she notices me staring at her with my mouth wide open. "Not that old people can't have sex."

My mouth snaps shut, and my eyes narrow on her. "Are you calling me old? Because I am not old enough to be your mother, which means I'm not old to you."

"But you are dating her dad who is old enough to be her mom." Suzie swishes her palms as if she's erasing her words. "Never mind. I don't know where my metaphor was going."

Max arrives and plops a plate of nachos on our table. "Why is Faith blushing?" He glares at his daughter. "I thought you didn't have a problem with us dating."

Hailey holds her hands up in surrender. "I don't! I went down a Prince Philip and Queen Elizabeth rabbit hole is all." She points to Suzie. "And she's not helping."

"Sell me down the river, why don't you?" Suzie accuses and then proceeds to show her best friend how it's done. "I'm not the one who called your dad's girlfriend old and told her she was too old for sex."

Max squeezes my shoulder. "You need me to rescue you?"

"I'm okay." His daughter and friend are the ones making fools of themselves. Not me.

"If you need me, just give me a sign."

"Should we work out some secret signal? I'll tug on my right ear if I need another wine and twitch my nose if I need help."

"Smart ass." He bends down and smacks my lips before moving off as if he didn't just kiss me in front of his daughter.

Hailey places her elbows on the table and sighs. "Watching Pops fall in love is my favorite thing."

Fall in love? I choke on my chip and end up downing my glass of wine to stop myself from choking to death. When I finally recover, I manage to say, "We're dating. No one's falling in love here."

"Tell it to someone who believes you," she sings. "Now, who wants to play some pool."

I look over at Max. His eyes are already on me. Despite him being a room away, I can see the heat in his eyes. Love? Nah. Lust? Oh yeah. That we have in spades.

Chapter 21

An amnesiac walks into a bar. He goes up to a beautiful young woman and asks, "Do I come here often?" ~ Text from Pops to Hailey

POPS

I drive like a maniac to get to the high school. I white-knuckle the wheel as I push through a barely still yellow light. I need to get to Ollie. The only thing the school secretary said was he's in trouble, and I need to come down to talk to the principal. I'm worried what the school calling me instead of Faith means. After all, I'm not Ollie's stepdad, although I'm working my way in that direction.

I call Faith's phone for the fifth time since I got in my car. No answer. Since I already left her a message, I hang up. Where could she be? I hope her past didn't catch up to her. I clench my jaw. I need to find her. I shake my head. No, she would want me to take care of her kid first. I put my fear and worries about Faith into a box and shut the lid.

Time to deal with Ollie's situation. I switch on the radio and tune in to the news. I pray there wasn't a school shooting. Ollie may not be mine, but it'd tear me apart if something happened to the kid. I release a breath I didn't realize I was holding when there's no news about a school shooting. I'm still on edge, though. There's a reason the school called me in, after all.

I drive into the high school parking lot and barely bring my truck to a stop in a guest parking spot before I jump out and race toward the entrance. After I make it through the rigamarole of the metal detector, I march to the front office. I know exactly where it is since Hailey graduated from this school.

"I'm Mr. McGraw. I'm here for Oliver Bakker."

"Please, have a seat," the secretary says. "The principal will be right with you."

Like I'm having a seat. "Where's Ollie? Is he okay?"

She purses her lips. "Like I said, the principal will be right with you."

I clench my jaw and fist my hands before I lose my patience. "Is my boy okay? Is he hurt?"

I hear a gasp behind me and spin around to see Ollie is right there sitting in a chair. I must have marched right past him when I walked in. When I see his eye is bruised and swollen, I nearly lose the thin hold I have on my temper. I wrestle my anger into control and kneel in front of him. "What happened?"

I don't give him a chance to answer before I'm standing and approaching the secretary again. "Why doesn't he have an ice pack?"

She frowns but heaves herself to her feet before clomping over to an office. She comes back a moment later with an instant ice pack. I take it from her and return to Ollie. I place it on his eye, and he winces. "Sorry, I know it hurts, but it will help with the swelling."

"Ma's gonna freak."

I pat his thigh. "We'll worry about her later. Did you have them call me because you were worried about her response?"

He shakes his head and winces with the movement. "They couldn't get a hold of her. You're not on my emergency contact list, but when she didn't answer for over an hour, they called you."

My jaw clenches. "You've been sitting here for an hour and no one offered you an ice pack or any pain relief?"

The principal's door opens. "Oliver Bakker," she says and motions us in.

I follow Ollie as he shuffles into the office.

"Max McGraw," I introduce myself to the woman. When Hailey attended school here, Mr. Stevens was the principal. He was a crotchety old man who didn't find my daughter's pranks amusing. He was obviously missing a sense of humor because Hailey's pranks were pretty awesome. I taught her myself.

"Principal Torres." She points to the chairs across from her desk, and we take our seats. I expect Ollie to start arguing, but he sits there and waits.

"What happened? Why weren't his wounds attended to before I arrived?"

Her brow wrinkles. "I wasn't aware he was injured."

I point to his face. "You can see the swelling and discoloration for yourself."

"My apologies. I was preoccupied."

If she thinks an apology will stop me from complaining, she's wrong. "And your secretary? She was sitting in front of him for the past hour and didn't move to help him."

"Again, my apologies. I'll speak to her." She clears her throat. "Now, if we can get to the matter at hand. Our school has a no violence policy. Ollie will be suspended for five days."

"No."

"Excuse me?" She raises an eyebrow in my direction. "No?"

"Have you looked at the kid? He has a black eye. And no wounds on his hands." I pick up his hands and show them to her. "If you took a minute to ask him what happened, I'm sure you'd learn he didn't commit any violence. Or are you suspending kids who are bullied now, too?"

"I wasn't bullied," Ollie claims.

"Attacked then," I amend.

Torres leans back in her chair and crosses her arms over her chest. "From what I understand, Oliver was not bullied or attacked. He instigated the incident."

"Bullshit," Ollie swears.

"Language," I correct.

"But it is bullshit. I didn't instigate a thing. A group of seniors were picking on this freshman girl. Making fun of her clothes and crowding her."

I growl. "Did they touch her?"

"They pushed her against a locker and blocked her from moving."

"Go on," I tell him when he pauses.

"I shouted for them to leave her alone. They asked me what I was going to do about it all by myself. I told them if they were going to pick on someone, they should pick on someone their own size. They released the girl to come at me, and the girl ran for help. By the time a teacher arrived, I had this." He points to his eye.

"It seems you haven't got the facts," I tell the principal.

Ollie snorts. "Of course not. The seniors are starters for the football team. No one cares what they do as long as they can play football."

The principal sighs and I know he hit a cord. "Do you have their names?"

"Better yet." He removes his phone from his pocket. "I've got video."

Torres buries her hands in her face. "Oh great. Have you posted it already?"

"Of course not. I'm not an idiot. This is my insurance policy."

My heart swells with pride as I listen to him. Ollie is one smart kid.

He fiddles with the phone. "I sent you an email with the video."

"I need to take care of this before we have a bigger mess on our hands," Principal Torres tells me.

I raise an eyebrow. "A bigger mess than senior boys assaulting a freshman girl?"

"Don't worry. I have proof now. Coach Howard won't have a leg to stand on this time."

The words 'this time' do not give me confidence on how these kids will be dealt with. Maybe it's time I teach Ollie how to fight.

"But I'd like for you to take Oliver home for the day until I can get a handle on the situation."

"Of course." I stand.

"And my apologies for my wrongful assumption."

Ollie shrugs. "No problem. A lot of people make wrongful assumptions about me," he says and damn near breaks my heart. I place my hand on his shoulder and steer him out of the office.

Ollie doesn't speak until we're in my truck heading to the bar. "Ma is going to lose it on me."

"We need to find her first."

"You don't know where she is either?" He bites his lip. "Do you think she's okay?"

Now that Ollie's safe, the box with my worry for Faith opens up. I clench my jaw to keep my emotions in check. I can't let her kid see how worried I am.

"She will be." I call Wally. "Faith's missing," is all I say when he answers.

"On it."

"Was that Wally?" Ollie asks. "Is he going to find Ma?"

"If anyone can, it's Wally."

I drive us to the pub since I don't know what's going on with Faith. I can feel the fear rolling off of Ollie in waves and force myself to keep a lid on my own fear. My brothers have been keeping an eye out for Faith since I discovered her reasons for moving to the city. They'll find her in no time. They have to.

"You hungry?" I ask when we walk into the pub. The place is mostly empty since the lunch crowd has come and gone.

"I can eat."

"Come on." I motion him to the kitchen and make him a burger and fries.

After I situate him at the bar with his food and a Coke, I check my phone. Damn it. No missed calls.

"Are you worried?" Ollie asks between bites of his burger.

"I'm sure your mom's fine. The battery on her phone is probably dead is all," I say instead of answering his question.

He rolls his eyes. "You can do a non-answer to a question as good as my mom."

I squeeze his shoulder. "Lots of practice, kid. Lots of practice."

"Did Hailey get in trouble all the time growing up?"

I don't get a chance to answer before the door flies open, and Faith rushes in. I let out the breath I've been holding for the past hour and give a chin lift to Wally who walks in behind her.

"What happened?" Faith asks as she rushes to Ollie. She lifts his head and winces when she sees the bruise. "What did you do?"

"He didn't do anything. He saved a girl from being attacked."

Faith's eyes close, and her head drops. "We're going to have to move again, aren't we? Maybe I should send you to a military school."

"It's okay, Ma. Pops talked to the principal and straightened everything out."

She looks over at me and places a hand over her heart. "Thank you."

"Not to pour oil on the fire, but we need to talk about teaching Ollie to fight."

Ollie rolls his eyes. "You did it now."

"I am not teaching him to fight."

I stand up tall and cross my arms over my chest. "No, I will."

"Don't forget about me," Wally adds.

"If you teach him to fight, he'll end up getting in more fights, which is the last thing I need," she argues.

I shake my head. "He needs to know how to defend himself. What if a teacher hadn't arrived after the first punch?" I point to Ollie's black eye.

She deflates, and Ollie elbows her. "You know they're right. Agent Judson said the same thing."

"Fine," she gives in.

"Now we've settled things. Where were you? Ollie was worried."

Ollie snorts. "And you weren't?"

I glare at him, and he laughs – the little shit.

"My car broke down, and my phone died while it was in for repair. The cord was in the car, and I couldn't charge my phone." She smiles at Wally. "Thanks for coming to get me, but how did you find me?"

Wally shakes his head. "Don't ask questions you don't want to know the answers to."

"I want to know," Ollie proclaims.

Wally strolls off with a flick of his hand and walks out of the bar without another word.

"You forgetting something, Spitfire?" I ask Faith once we're alone in the place.

She wrinkles her brow. "I don't think I am."

I shake my head. "Get over here and greet me properly."

"Not in front of the kid," she whisper-shouts.

"It's fine." Ollie stands with his plate and walks off to the pool tables.

And I'm done waiting. I round the bar and gather her into my arms. I kiss her until she melts. "You scared the crap out of me," I admit.

"Right back at ya."

"This situation in Saint Louis needs to be taken care of."

I'm done waiting for the FBI or police or whoever in Saint Louis to figure this out. It's time to take action.

Chapter 22

A minister, a priest, and a rabbi walk into a bar. "What is this," asks the bartender, "some kind of joke?" ~ Text from Pops to Hailey

POPS

I pace behind the bar as I wait for my brothers to arrive. I wasn't kidding when I told Faith the situation in Saint Louis needs to be resolved. I am done with her living in fear. I'm ready to move on to the next stage with her, but I know she won't move forward with this hanging over her head.

The door bangs open, and Wally, Sid, Barney, and Lenny walk in.

"Hey," Barney begins, and I cringe. Here we go. "Why did god give men penises?" He snickers as he waits for someone to guess an answer, but no one bothers to reply. "So they'd have at least one way to shut a woman up."

He guffaws and slaps his thigh.

Sid shakes his head. "Brother, your game needs work if that's the only way you know to get a woman to shut up."

"I think Sid has news for us," Wally says in response to Sid's bragging.

Sid glares at him. "Fucker. I told you to stop it with the spying on me."

"What's going on?" I ask before the two can get into a fistfight.

You'd think Wally could annihilate Sid in a fight since he's still doing his black ops shit for the government. But Sid can give him a run for his money. It doesn't hurt that Sid doesn't fight fair. The man grew up with a single mom and had to learn early on how to fight when his mom's boyfriends thought they could take their fists to him.

Sid stops glaring at Wally to grin my way. "I'm getting married."

Lenny slaps him on the back. "Congrats, brother." Then, he holds out his hand to Barney. "Pay up."

"I was sure Mary Ann wouldn't take you back after she caught you flirting with those sorority girls," Barney whines.

Sid smirks and rolls back on his heels. "It was only a bit of innocent flirting."

Barney rolls his eyes. "Yeah, right."

Sid's smirk drops from his face. "What the hell, man? You know I'm not a cheater."

"There's cheating and then there's cheating."

"Flirting is not cheating."

I rub a hand over my face before reining this shit in. "When's the big day?"

"Two weeks."

"What do you buy as a gift for someone's sixth wedding?" Wally asks.

Barney raises his hand. "I know. A divorce lawyer."

I manage to catch Sid as he launches himself at Barney. I wrap my arms around his middle and drag him away. "You know he's trying to get a rise out of you. And you're letting him."

Sid's nostrils flare as he eyeballs Barney. If I didn't have business to attend to, I'd let Sid have him. Barney's rubbing salt in an open wound and he knows it. Sid's first wife was the love of his life, but she couldn't handle him being a deployed soldier. He promised to get out of the Army as soon as he could, but she didn't wait. He arrived home from Iraq to find she'd packed her stuff and taken off.

But Sid isn't a man who can be alone. He likes having a woman at home he can spoil. Unfortunately, he also likes to do whatever he wants and often forgets to tell his wife where he's at. He might never cheat, but he doesn't instill a whole lot of trust in his partners either.

"Congratulations," I tell him in a bid to get him to calm down.

His smile stretches from ear to ear, and there's a twinkle in his eyes. Maybe Mary Ann is the one who will stick. It doesn't hurt she's an ER nurse who works all kinds of crazy hours and won't be sitting at home wondering where Sid is when he forgets to call.

"If we're done with this touching moment, can we move on to the agenda for the day? Where's Ollie?" Wally asks and looks down the hallway as if expecting the kid to walk out any second.

We're standing in my bar in the middle of the day. "Why would Ollie be here?"

Wally bounces on his toes. "Because we need to teach him how to fight."

Sid cracks his knuckles. "Yeah, no punk seniors are going to give our kid a black eye again."

Barney shakes his head. "This is a change from Hailey. When she was in high school, we had to worry about her beating kids up all the time."

Lenny frowns. "Don't underestimate the kid. I'm sure he could put a beat down on someone if he wanted to. But he's a good kid."

"Where is he?" Wally pushes. "We're ready to get this show on the road."

Now I understand why they came dressed in sweats instead of their usual jeans, plaid shirts, and scuffed boots.

"I didn't ask you to come here today to teach Ollie how to fight," I explain.

Sid frowns. "Why are we here then?"

Wally answers for me. "Because he's ready to step in and solve the Saint Louis situation."

Lenny walks to the bar. "I need a beer for this conversation."

I walk behind the bar and tap beers for the group of them before pouring myself a coke. I need a clear head for this conversation.

"Now," I begin once everyone has a drink. "Does anyone have any ideas on how to deal with those bastards in Saint Louis?"

"What did the agent in charge say?" Wally asks.

I frown. "Judson said the same thing he's been telling Faith for a while now. No one's looking for Ollie, but he's worried the truce between the gangs will blow sky high if Ollie shows up."

"By which he means he's afraid the kid will be targeted again if they return," Wally interprets, and I nod in agreement.

"What do you want us to do?" Sid asks.

"We can go down there and kick some gang ass." Lenny rubs his hands together. "I haven't given someone a good ass-kicking in a while now."

Barney shoves his shoulder. "As if you could ever give anyone a good ass-kicking."

"While I'm all for some ass-kicking." I'd love to go down there and kick the asses of those douchebags who thought it was okay to rape a young girl. "I don't think violence is the answer."

Barney snickers. "You sound like your wife now."

I don't correct him when he calls Faith my wife because she will be my wife. But first, we need to take care of this situation.

Lenny slaps a twenty on the bar. "I've got two months before Faith is his wife."

Barney takes out his wallet. "Sucker. Six months." He slaps a bill down.

Sid rubs his jaw as he studies me. I cross my arms over my chest and let him look his fill. "One month."

"No way. We won't have the situation solved in a month. I say a year." Wally places his money on top of the pile of bills.

"Are you fuckers done now?" I ask.

Lenny laughs. "This is great. Who knew Pops falling in love was going to end up financing my new bike?"

"Don't count your chickens before your eggs hatch," Sid says.

Lenny puffs up his chest. "Have I or have I not won all the bets thus far?"

I reach across the bar and smack him upside the head. "Enough with the bets about my love life."

"Which reminds me," he says, "we need details on what happened in the hotel room at Phoebe's wedding."

He barely moves in time to miss my fist. "Enough!" I slam my fist down on the bar to make my point perfectly fucking clear.

"Maybe we should move on before the vein in Pops' forehead pops," Wally suggests.

I take deep breaths until I feel my jaw relax and the blood returns to my fisted hands. "Does anyone else have any ideas on how to solve the Saint Louis situation?"

All eyes look to Wally. He frowns. "I can handle it, but it's going to take a while."

No one questions his ability to take care of the situation, and no one asks how he will take care of it. We know better than to ask.

"I owe you."

Wally scowls. "You don't owe me. I'm not doing this for you. I'm doing it for our kid Ollie."

I wonder if Ollie realizes he just gained four uncles who will scorch the earth to keep him safe. I'll set up a time for the guys to teach Ollie some self-defense. He needs to know he has men who will have his back. I don't think he's had a whole lot of adult male mentoring these past years.

"But, brother, I need you to consider something."

I lift my chin at Wally to continue.

"If I solve the situation in Saint Louis, Faith is going to want to move back there. But you can't leave. You have the bar here."

As if I haven't already thought of this contingency and made my decision. "I'll sell the bar and follow her."

I hear a gasp and whip my head around to see who it is. Damn it. Faith is standing there with her eyes bulging, and her mouth hanging open. This is not how I wanted her to learn how serious I am about her.

"Pay up, fuckers," Wally says. "I told you he loves her."

Chapter 23

Hey, train wreck! This isn't your station.

LIKE AN IDIOT, I stand in the doorway of McGraw's Pub and stare with my mouth hanging open at Max. Would he seriously sell the bar and move to Saint Louis to be with me? Is he crazy? The bar isn't merely his livelihood, it's his life. His friends hang out here all the time, and he lives in the apartment above. And then there's his daughter. He can't possibly want to leave her.

Max's brothers shuffle over to me. "Good to see you, doll," Lenny says and pats my shoulder before squeezing past me.

Barney pats my other shoulder. "See ya, Faith."

Sid grins and wraps me in a hug. "Welcome to the family."

Welcome to the family? My stomach warms at the idea of having somewhere to belong, but my head rejects the sentiment. They can't seriously think I'm family.

Wally plucks me from Sid's arms. "We're going to fix this and make you and Ollie safe."

Pressure builds behind my eyes, and I have to blink to keep the tears from falling. "This is what family does," he whispers to me. "They take care of one another. Go easy on Max, will ya?"

I nod, but I have no idea why I'm nodding.

Once the men have filed out of the bar, I turn around to find Max standing in front of me. He's not quite fidgeting, but a muscle is ticking in his jaw.

"Do you want to talk about this?"

At his question, the warm feelings his brothers caused flee. "Are you out of your mind?"

He tags my hand and drags me away from the doorway down the hallway to his office. He sits on the sofa and arranges me on his lap until I'm straddling him. I do not want to have this conversation while straddling him. As if I can think of anything else than stripping him naked and licking him like a fudgsicle when he's this close.

I push on his shoulders and try to get to my feet. He stops me. "Please, I need for you to be in my arms when I tell you this."

I relent. How can I not? His deep, husky voice brings up memories of when he was whispering dirty things to me while we were in Phoebe's honeymoon suite. My body heats, and I feel myself get excited at those memories.

"I lied to you."

"What?" I push against him and try to leverage myself to my feet, but he wraps his arms around my shoulders and keeps me imprisoned in his arms. Alrighty then. I guess I'm screaming in his face. "How dare you? I've had enough of men lying to me to last several lifetimes. I don't need you to lie to me, too."

When I see the smirk on his face, I'm tempted to smack it right off of him. But no. Violence is not the answer. Although I'm mighty tempted to revert my stand on it right now.

"You're gorgeous when you're mad, Spitfire."

"Are you serious right now? Did you hit your head one too many times?"

"Shall I explain before you perform a beat down on me?" I can feel his chest move with silent laughter.

"You're certifiable." I squirm, but he doesn't loosen his hold on me.

"I said I was falling in love with you. It was a lie."

I freeze. He lied? He's not falling in love with me? And why isn't it a relief to hear those words? I don't want a man to fall in love with me, I remind myself. Except I know perfectly well I'm feeding myself bull cocky.

He bends forward and whispers into my ear, "I'm not falling. I'm there."

The butterflies in my stomach shout hallelujah and start performing cartwheels. Since when can butterflies do cartwheels? Shouldn't they be flapping their wings? And why am I thinking about butterflies? Oh yeah, because I'm terrified to consider what Max's words mean.

"We agreed this was a short-term fling," I claim.

"When did we agree to that?"

I ignore his question because he's right. We never agreed to have a short-term fling. It's only me who's assumed our relationship had an expiration date since I know my time in the city is limited, but I never actually said the words out loud to him.

"I can't think long-term," I tell him instead of answering his question. "I'm a single mom. I need to concentrate on my son."

"Ollie's fifteen, nearly sixteen. He's not a toddler you have to watch every second of the day."

"Maybe not, but I need to ensure he makes it through high school and is ready for college."

"He's a straight A student. He's ready for college. Considering all the advanced placement courses he's taking, I wouldn't be surprised if he could skip an entire year of college."

Why does he have to be all reasonable when I'm having a freak-out and being completely unreasonable? It's not fair! I slap his chest. "You're not hearing me."

He captures my hands. "I am hearing you. I hear you're scared and afraid to take a chance, but you have nothing to fear from me. I'm standing at the bottom of the cliff waiting to catch you with open arms."

"But Ollie," I say because we're a package deal.

"I'll catch him, too. Hell, my brothers have already officially adopted him."

"They have?" I shake my head. No, it's too much to hope for. If things don't work out between Max and I, it would crush Ollie to lose them.

He growls. "Stop it. Things are going to work out. But do you think those men give a crap about our relationship?"

I roll my eyes. "Um, yeah. They're taking bets on us constantly."

He grins. "Not what I meant, and you know it. My brothers will be an uncle to your son no matter what the status of our relationship is. I didn't go to them and ask them to take the kid on. They're the ones who brought him into the fold."

"They are?"

"Your kid went up against five kids who are bigger than him to protect a girl yesterday. My brothers would burn the world down to keep him safe. They all showed up here today to give him lessons in self-defense."

My nose wrinkles. "But he's in school right now."

"Doesn't matter to them. I called, and they came running because they thought Ollie needed their help."

My heart warms with affection for his friends. "But we're here temporarily."

"And I will follow you wherever you go," he declares.

My heart goes flippity-floppity. I place my hand over it in case it decides to bounce straight out of my chest into Max's hands.

Max's eyes drop to my lips, and he leans in. I place a hand over his mouth. "No, we need to talk about this."

He shrugs. "What's there to talk about?"

And boom! My anger is ignited once again. "What's there to talk about?" I shriek. "You can't give up your entire life for me!"

"I can if I want to. And trust me, sweetheart, I want to. I'm fifty-six years old. I've been waiting to find the love of my life a hell of a long time. I'm not letting anything stand in my way."

Holy cow does the man know how to do romance. Considering he's been alone most of his life, it's pretty much a miracle. But I'm not there. I have my son and the whole catastrophe in Saint Louis to think of.

"But—"

He shushes me. "I know you're not there yet. I don't like it, but I understand. All I ask is for you to give us a chance. Take this day by day and see where it leads."

"What if we can move back to Saint Louis?"

"Then, sweetheart, we'll deal with it on the day it happens. There's no sense twisting ourselves into pretzels about it right now since it's not safe for you to return anyway."

I drop my head and fidget with the button of his plaid shirt. I'm terrified to take it day by day. Each day I spend with him, my heart attaches more and more to him. I'm afraid when it's time to leave the city my heart will be fused to his and refuse to release him. But I can't stay here. It's not fair to Ollie. And I can't ask Max to come with us.

Max places a finger under my chin and lifts my head. "Hey. We don't need to figure everything out today, sweetheart. We have time."

And then his head descends, and his lips meet mine, and I forget all about the reasons this is a terrible mistake and let my body feel the delicious things he does to me.

Chapter 24

As a parent, my day job runs from 'startled awake'
to 'passed out on the couch'.

MAX STANDS WITH ME in his arms. "Not here. I want to take my time with you and not worry someone on my staff will come bursting through the door any minute."

He carries me to his apartment above the bar. I've been up here once before when Ollie found a bunch of kittens, and Max agreed to foster the litter until homes could be found. I should have known then I had no chance to keep my distance from this man.

"I can walk, you know," I protest as he carries me into his apartment.

"Can but don't have to."

I give in and look around his place instead. The kitchen and living room are in one large, open space. It has a loft feel to it with visible brick walls, high ceilings, and exposed ducts overhead. The kitchen is surprisingly large considering he can get food from downstairs whenever he wants.

Max doesn't slow down and keeps marching straight to his bedroom where he lays me down on his bed. The loft feel continues in his room with floor-to-ceiling windows, more exposed brick, and minimal furniture. Besides the bed, there are two nightstands and nothing else.

It doesn't feel cold, though. There are colorful rugs on the floor I know Hailey must have picked out, and one of the walls is covered with pictures of Hailey and his brothers. On the other wall is a massive television. The bed itself is king-sized and covered in a dark-gray down comforter.

"You done checking out my place?"

At Max's question, I realize I'm gawking. "Sorry, but it's gorgeous."

"I'll give you a tour later. We have more important matters to deal with now."

"Oh yeah?" I tease. "Like what?"

He licks his lips but doesn't answer my question verbally. Instead, his hands lift, and he starts unbuttoning his flannel shirt. I sit up. I like this show. His pecs are revealed and then his abs. I think I may be drooling. I want to get my hands and mouth on him in the worst way.

"Are you sure you're a fifty-something dad and not an alien of some sort?"

He chuckles before kneeling on the bed.

"Aren't you going to take the rest of your clothes off?" I protest. "I was enjoying the show."

"You first, sweetheart."

I decide I'm done listening to men. I sit up and launch myself at him. I catch him off guard and manage to get him on his back with me on top.

"It's my turn."

He opens his arms wide. "Have at it, sweetheart."

I meld my lips to his and allow his sweet and spicy taste to fill me. I could kiss him all day, but I have other needs to attend to. I end the kiss and move my lips down his jaw to his neck. His skin tastes fresh and salty reminding me of the beach in the summer. I lick his skin until I reach the joint between his shoulder and neck where I nibble him with my teeth.

Max moans and his hands move to the hem of my sweater. He tugs on it until I lift up, and he tosses it away. His hands move to cover my breasts, but I stop him.

"Tsk. Tsk. It's my turn now."

He moans. "Please let me touch you."

"You'll have your chance."

I return to exploring his body with my tongue. He has a smattering of hair on his chest. I run my hands through it and tug lightly before moving on to his nipples. From prior experience, I know his nipples are ultra-sensitive. Time to use this information to my advantage. I swipe my tongue around the area until he groans. Then, I strike and bite him. His back bows off the bed and his hands find my head. He threads his fingers through my hair and uses his hold to keep me right where he wants me. I obey for a while by nibbling and licking the area, but then it's time to continue my exploration.

I run my tongue down the center of his chest until I come to his jeans. I lift my head and wink at him. "Someone is wearing entirely too many clothes."

"I guess you need to rectify the situation then."

Oh, I will. I unbutton his jeans and open them to reveal his hard length encased in a pair of tight black boxer briefs. I run my finger up and down his length and grin when I see it jump in response. Max growls, and I look up to see he's moved his hands and he's now gripping his headboard hard enough his knuckles have turned white.

I can't believe little old me is making this man lose his control, but I'm not stupid. I'm going to take advantage while I can. I peel his underwear down and his cock pops out. Precum is already leaking from the head. My tongue darts out and I lick it off.

He pants. "You don't have to."

"But what if I want to?"

I don't wait for his response and take his length into my mouth. I bob up and down once before releasing him to let my tongue trace the pulsing vein down his shaft until I come to his balls. I draw one into my mouth and suck while my hand massages the other one. I release him with a pop and move back to the main attraction.

I draw his length into my mouth again while using my hands to fist the area my mouth can't reach. I twist my wrist and Max groans. I suck as I bob my head up and down several times. I'm enjoying the way he tastes in my mouth when I feel Max's abs contract before he jackknifes up and grabs me under my arms. He throws me down on the bed and climbs on top of me.

"Were you trying to make me lose control?" His voice is husky. The sound makes tingles erupt throughout my body and the ache below intensify. I rub my legs together to relieve the ache.

Max notices the movement and smirks. He crawls down my body until his face is level with my jeans. "Time for these to go," he mutters as he undoes them and drags them down my legs. He takes his time, and I squirm. I'm ready for the main attraction to begin. I unsnap my bra and let it fall open.

"Patience," he admonishes.

He draws his hands along my legs as he crawls up my body. When he reaches the tops of my thighs, he uses his hands to spread my legs and settles himself between them. Right where I want him. His cock bumps my clit, and I moan as my head falls back. I arch my back and rub my chest against his until I feel my nipples harden.

Max slides his cock up and down my slit, but he doesn't enter me. I'm about ready to yell at him to get the show going when he freezes.

"Fuck. Condom." He lifts up, but I wrap my legs around him to keep him where he is.

"It's okay. I'm clean."

"I get tested each year for my annual physical. I'm clean, too," he tells me. "But are you sure?"

I bob my head. I'm not about to let him move away from me. I am more than ready to have sex for the first time in an embarrassingly long time. Except for him going down on me at Phoebe's wedding, which is a memory I'll cherish for a lifetime.

Instead of entering me like I want, Max drops his head and takes my breast into his mouth. Each tug of his mouth causes a spasm down below, and I moan. I tighten my legs around his waist and try to force him to move to where I need him, but he doesn't budge. He takes his time lavishing one breast before moving onto the other.

I'm gyrating against him and using all of my strength to push him to where I want him when he finally pops my breast out of his mouth. "Love these," he murmurs.

I'm too out of my mind with need to respond to his ridiculous statement. "Good. Now, move." I punctuate my words by rotating my hips.

He chuckles but doesn't hesitate to notch his cock into position. His head raises and he looks me in the eyes as he slowly fills me. I can't deal with the adoration I see there and let my head fall back and just feel. I forgot how good this feels. How good it feels to have a man above you pumping slowly in and out of you.

"Fuck, Faith. You feel too good. I won't last."

I raise my head to look at him. The muscles in his neck strain as he tries to maintain control. I did that. I made this man fight for his control. The thought causes my excitement to build and liquid to gush from me. In response, Max groans and his pace quickens.

Warmth builds in my stomach. No, I fight it. I don't want to come already. I don't want this moment to ever end. Max speeds up the pace of his thrusts even more, and I become powerless to fight the build-up. Tingles begin in my core and travel throughout my body until I'm shouting, "Yes, yes, yes!"

"Say my name, sweetheart. Say my name," he grunts.

I manage to lift my head and look him in the eye as I cry, "Max."

His thrusts become chaotic. "Faith!" He grunts before I feel a gush of warmth fill me. His thrusts slow until they stop altogether. He collapses on me but rolls quickly to my side and tucks me into him. He kisses my hair. "I love you, Faith."

My heart skips a beat before it starts beating like a drum. Thump. Thump. Thump. I know he said he'd fallen for me, but I was ignoring his words. But I can't ignore an I love you. Shit. Shit. Shit.

I jump from the bed and search for my clothes. "I can't, Max. I told you. I can't."

"Stop running scared."

"I'm not running scared."

"You sure as hell are. I've had one wife who didn't stick around. I'm not going to deal with another."

His words pierce through me like a dagger to my heart. My hands freeze from zipping up my pants. "Is that what you think? I'm like your ex-wife?" Not one single person has had a nice thing to say about his ex. If there's one person in the world I don't want to ever be compared to, it's her.

He rubs a hand over his face. "I didn't mean it the way it sounded."

His words, an excuse I've heard a million times before, spur me into finishing dressing. "I guess this makes things easy then. If you think I'm like your ex-wife, there's nothing for us to discuss."

With those parting words, I rush out of his apartment as fast as my legs can take me. I hear him jump up and chase after me, but he's naked. He doesn't have a chance of catching me. I sniff but I don't let the first tear fall until I'm locked in my car and driving out of the parking lot. I won't let another man break me.

Chapter 25

My son told me I was being overdramatic, so I changed the Wi-Fi password. Let's see who's being overdramatic in about five minutes.

"WHAT'S WRONG WITH YOU?"

At Ollie's question, I blink my eyes and return to the present where I'm sitting on the sofa in our living room staring at the television. The television I forgot to switch on. Who needs to watch a tv program when you have a film of how royally you messed up your life on repeat in your head?

"Nothing," I tell him. Lying to your kid is allowed when you're protecting him from your emotional wreckage.

"Yeah, right." He snorts. "Did you get into a fight with Pops?"

My lips turn down. I don't think I like how perceptive the kid is. "When did you get to be this smart?"

"I've always been this smart."

I roll my eyes and then attack. I wrap my arm around his head and give him a noogie.

"Ma," he whines. "Cut it out."

I giggle and free him. When I calm down, I notice the time is after six. Time to get off my lazy ass and feed my kid. My stomach rumbles. And myself, I guess. As I walk to the kitchen, there's a knock on the door.

"I've got it."

Ollie rushes to the door before I can stop him. I make a U-turn and follow him. I'm surprised to see Aiden standing in the doorway of my apartment.

"What are you doing here?" Oops. Can I be any ruder? "Sorry. Rewind. Hi, Aiden. How are you?"

He grins. "Hi, Faith. I'm wondering if I can steal Ollie for the night." At my obvious look of confusion, he explains, "We're having poker night at my place and thought he might like to join us."

Ollie tugs on my sleeve. "Can I, Ma? Can I, please?"

"We haven't had dinner yet."

"No worries. We're ordering pizza," Aiden says, and Ollie cheers. Aiden had to say pizza, didn't he?

"He has an eleven o'clock bedtime on Fridays."

Ollie's face turns bright red. "Maaaaa," he whines.

"What? It's true."

Aiden lifts his hands in a placating gesture. "No problem. I'll have him home by eleven."

"I guess it's all right then." I ruffle Ollie's hair. "But—"

Ollie cuts me off. "Listen to my elders, be polite, and no alcohol." He rushes out the door and motions for Aiden to hurry up.

"Thanks, Faith," Aiden says before he follows Ollie.

Once I'm alone, I contemplate what to do about dinner. I'd love to order pizza, but Ollie's college fund isn't going to magically grow on its own. It's barely growing as it is. I'm banging around the cupboards when there's another knock on the door. It's Grand Central Station in here today.

"What now?" I ask as I open the door. "Sorry," I say when I see Hailey, Suzie, and Phoebe standing there. "I thought Aiden and Ollie returned."

"I've been confused for a boy before," Suzie says. "But never a hot man. I'm not sure how to respond."

It's best to ignore Suzie's craziness. "What's up?"

"Can we come in?" Hailey asks and holds up two grocery bags. "We brought supplies."

I narrow my eyes on her but open the door wide to let them in. "What's going on?" I ask once the door's closed and Ms. Snoop down the hall can't hear us.

"We came to cheer you up!" Suzie announces with her hands raised like she's going to literally start cheering to cheer me up.

I cross my arms over my chest and stare her down. "Cheer me up? What for?"

Hailey places a hand on my back and pushes me toward the sofa. "Come on. Sit down. And we'll explain."

I huff but take a seat. "I'm down. Explain."

Hailey rocks on her heels before plowing forth. "We know you and Pops had a fight. We're here as your girl posse to cheer you up."

"And to bitch out Pops," Suzie adds.

Phoebe's face pales. "As long as there's no talk about s-e-x."

"What are you spelling for?" Suzie asks. "Everyone here knows how to spell sex. Hell, even Ollie knows how to spell sex, but he's at Aiden's."

I slap my forehead. "I should have known there was something going on when Aiden showed to take Ollie away for the night."

"You'll thank me later," Hailey sings. "Now, where do you want the groceries?"

Since my kid isn't here to see me make a mess, I dive into the bags in the living room. I remove five bags of chips, a box of cookies, some brownies, and a pint of ice cream from one bag. The other bag is full of wine, beer, and vodka.

My eyes widen as I look around at all the food. "I haven't had a night like this with friends in forever."

Hailey clears her throat. "Let's get the serious stuff over before we dig into the food and let the man bashing begin."

"I'm not going to man bash," Phoebe protests.

Suzie places a hand over her heart. "Look at our little girl, all loved up. You should have met her when she first arrived."

"We don't talk about Phoebe 1.0."

"Guys." Hailey claps her hands. "We're getting off topic here."

I raise my hand. "What is the topic again?"

"You and my dad."

I should have kept my fool mouth shut.

"Yeah. What happened?" Suzie asks. "Did Pops not perform in the bedroom? Talk about a disappointment. I imagine he has a righteous sized love rod. It would be a shame to hear he doesn't know how to use it."

My mouth opens and words come out before my mind catches up. "Don't worry. He knows how to use it." I slap a hand over my mouth as my face heats. "Holy firecracker. Ignore what I just said."

Suzie leans close. "I'm not ignoring a thing. Give me more. I want all the deets."

Phoebe looks green. "Please, no details about your sex life with Pops."

Hailey giggles. "He's my dad. I'm the one who should look like she's about to upchuck on her fancy Loubobo shoes, not you."

"It's Louboutins," Phoebe corrects as she places a hand over her middle and gulps like she's trying to keep the contents of her stomach inside her body.

I can't resist teasing. "I guess I shouldn't tell you about the thing he does with his tongue."

Phoebe gags and I burst out laughing. "I'm teasing. There is no thing with his tongue."

"Now, I'm disappointed," Suzie grumps.

"All right, kids, quiet down. Quiet down," Hailey orders. "I can recognize avoidance when I see it," she tells me. "If you don't want to talk about what's wrong, we'll leave you alone."

"Hey!" Suzie shouts, but Hailey ignores her.

She places a hand on my thigh. "But we're here for you if you do want to talk."

"Yeah." Phoebe nods in agreement. "We've all been there."

"Yup." Even Suzie agrees. "Men get their heads up their asses and we need to help pull them out."

"Ugh!" I bury my face in my hands. "It's not Max who has his head up his ass. It's me."

Hailey pries my hands away from my face. "What happened?"

"He compared me to your mom, and I lost my mind." I squeeze her hands. "Please tell me I'm nothing like her." My eyes widen when I realize what I said. "Ignore me. Being friendly with your boyfriend's daughter is complicated."

Phoebe snorts. "You want complicated? How about falling in love with the man who kidnapped you?"

Hailey kneels in front of me. "My mom was nothing like you. You literally gave up your entire life to keep your kid safe. My mom never attended one of my performances, let alone remembered my birthday. She was nothing like you."

"Totally!" Suzie agrees. "Why would Pops compare you to her? Sounds like he has his head firmly lodged up his ass."

"I kind of freaked out about something he said and when I started to leave, he told me to stop running and said he wouldn't deal with another woman who wouldn't stick around."

Hailey gasps. "He said that?"

Suzie stands. "I'm going to kick his ass. Where's your baseball bat?"

Hailey joins Suzie, and they look like they're about to march out of my apartment to go confront Max. Phoebe stands and holds up her hands. "Hold up. What happened then? Did you ask him to explain?"

"No, I ran out of there like my ass was on fire."

"Then, maybe he didn't mean it like it sounded and you need to give him a chance to explain."

"I don't like this voice of reason stuff," Suzie announces. "Can't we kick ass now and demand explanations later?"

Hailey sighs. "I hate to say it, but Phoebe's right." At Suzie's gasp, she explains, "It's the adult thing to do. Ask him to explain himself. If he still compares you to my mom, we'll kick his ass."

"And I'll join them," Phoebe says.

Suzie grunts and stomps back to us. She throws herself into the armchair. "Fine!" Hailey ruffles her hair as she passes and joins me on the sofa.

"Now." Phoebe rubs her hands together. "I want to hear what Pops said to make Faith lose her mind and run away like a high school girl who just found out she's pregnant with her math teacher's baby."

Suzie narrows her eyes at Phoebe. "That's an awfully specific example."

"Shush. I want to hear what Pops said."

My heart skips a beat as I remember the words Max uttered. *I love you, Faith.* No. I shake my head. I'm not ready to figure out how I feel about him declaring his love, let alone dissect the information with his daughter and her friends.

"Hard pass," I say.

Hailey studies me for a long moment before giving in. "Time to eat. Who wants what on their pizza?"

We order pizza and drink wine while watching overly romantic movies. Suzie boos the television and throws food at it while Hailey makes a running commentary on everything they got wrong about the soldier in the show. I remain quiet as I stuff my face.

My eyes are on the television, but my mind is full of the task I've kind of agreed to perform. I need to let Max explain himself. I don't want to. Deep down I know he doesn't think I'm like his ex-wife, but I latched onto his words as an excuse to run the second he uttered those scary love words.

I take another sip of wine and push thoughts of Max out of my head. Tomorrow. I'll deal with him and everything else tomorrow.

Chapter 26

Eighty percent of being a mom is telling your son "wow that's cool" without bothering to look.

SATURDAY IS THE DAY of Sid's wedding. Since I can't avoid Max during the day without ruining Sid and his bride's special day – not to mention looking like a total dork – I decide it's time to be an adult and message Max to ask him to meet me in advance to talk. He responds that he'll be at the coffee shop down the street from McGraw's.

Ollie and I arrive ten minutes early, but Max is already waiting outside on the sidewalk for us. He's dressed in a gray charcoal suit fitted to his broad shoulders and tapered waist. My belly flutters as I take in how good he fills out the outfit.

"Faith." He nods but makes no move to touch me, and damn, does his nonchalance hurt. I caused this myself, though. I have no reason to complain. I straighten my back. I can do this.

"Max. Thanks for coming."

He opens the door and motions us inside.

"Straighten her out," Ollie says before wandering off to find a table of his own.

I stare after him with my mouth hanging open. "When did my teenager skip puberty and move straight to adulthood?"

"Come on." Max places his hand on my back and leads me to the counter. "Let's buy you one of those coffees which is more chocolate than coffee and then we can talk."

After we get our drinks, we find an empty corner with a free table. I take a sip of coffee and wait for Max to speak, but when he remains quiet, I realize I'm the one who needs to start this party.

"You said you wanted to explain?" Although now I think about it, he didn't say those words exactly.

Max clears his throat. "First of all, I'm sorry if it sounded like I was comparing you to my ex-wife. I didn't mean to. Lucy couldn't hold a candle to you."

"Then why did you bring her up," I lean forward and whisper, "when I was naked?"

I know I sound like a total dork, but being naked while being compared to his ex-wife was like adding a rotten cherry to the top of a spoiled sundae.

He runs a hand over his mouth. "I'm sorry. I guess I over-reacted when your response to my declaration of love was to immediately jump out of bed."

At his mention of what he said, I have to grasp the table to stop myself from rushing straight out of here. I look down at my knuckles turning white from how hard I'm holding onto the table. Well, shit. He's right. I was running scared. I want to run scared right now in fact. I'm a big fat scaredy-cat. Meow!

Max reaches across the table and pries one of my hands loose. "I'm sorry, sweetheart. I pushed too far too fast. I know I should treat you more carefully."

"I'm not made of spun glass," I snap.

"Of course not."

I frown at him. "Don't placate me."

He holds up his hands in surrender. "Sorry."

"Still placating."

He shakes his head. "Will you forgive me for being an ass? I can't promise never to be an ass again. I'm a man after all, and this is my first relationship since my ex left. I'm bound to be rusty and say stupid stuff from time to time."

How can I not forgive him? I'm nearly as much at fault as he is and here he is apologizing while I'm still thinking about running out of here as fast as I can. I sigh. "I forgive you as long as you can forgive me for being a flight risk."

"I get it. You're protecting your heart. I need to prove you can trust me. Then, you can give me your heart knowing I'll take care of it."

His words turn me to mush. Darn him. "How are you this good at the romance thing when you've been single for two decades?"

He winks. "I've been saving all the romance for you, Spitfire."

I roll my eyes. "You went from romantic to corny in the blink of an eye."

Ollie walks over and stops at our table. "I'm guessing by the mushy look in Ma's eyes, you made up. You ready to go? Aiden texted to ask where we are."

My brow wrinkles. "Aiden is texting you now?"

"Give it a rest, Ma," Ollie says.

We stand, and Max takes my hand in his. Since Sid is having his wedding reception at McGraw's, we walk the short distance to the pub. Ollie rushes in before us. I move to catch him, but Max stops me.

"He's safe here. All my brothers are inside."

"Sorry. I'm not used to having help taking care of him."

He throws his arm over my shoulders and squeezes. "You have all the help you need now."

We walk inside and pause right inside the doorway to allow our eyes to adjust to the dim lighting.

Hailey claps. "Yeah! They made up."

Suzie grunts. "Damn. I was looking forward to pulling his head out of his ass."

"Is that why you got the baseball bat out this morning? You said you were joining a softball league." Suzie looks up at her husband and winks. Grayson shakes his head. "You are such a troublemaker."

"And yet you married me anyway."

Considering how often Suzie says those words, I think she's finding it hard to believe the man she loves married her. I look up at Max. I get where she's coming from.

We gather at the bar, and I look around the group. "Where's Sid?"

Max consults his watch. "He should be here any moment."

As if Max and Sid orchestrated the entire thing, the door opens, and Sid enters carrying a woman in his arms. She slaps his shoulder. "Put me down, you big oaf. You're supposed to carry me over the threshold of our home, not a bar."

"Considering how much time he spends here, it's his second home," Max mutters.

Sid lets his bride down, and the group mobs them. I hang back for a moment and wait for my chance. I study Sid's bride, Mary Ann, as I wait. She's tall – easily as tall as Phoebe who is five-foot-nine – with dark, curly hair and olive skin. She's the perfect dark to Sid's light blond looks.

"How do you turn a fox into an elephant?" Barney asks as I join them.

Sid glares, but Barney isn't deterred. "You marry it!"

Sid pushes Mary Ann behind him and confronts Barney. "I won't have you telling crass jokes to my bride."

Mary Ann pushes past him. "Is this why you haven't introduced me to your friends before? You're worried I can't handle a little teasing?" She laughs. "I handle you all right, don't I?"

Sid blushes. "Yeah, you sure do."

Barney raises his hand, and Mary Ann high-fives him. Sid wraps an arm around her waist and pulls her near. "You're supposed to be on my side," he grumbles.

Hailey laughs. "No wonder you've been married—" She cuts herself off. "Sorry. I'm Hailey. Sid's my uncle," she introduces.

Max arrives with a tray of champagne glasses. Everyone takes a glass and raises them to the happy couple.

"Welcome back everyone," Barney starts his toast, and Max thumps him on his back hard enough he loses his balance.

"Sorry, Mary Ann, I couldn't resist," he acts contrite but there's a twinkle in his eye. Knowing Barney, he's been waiting to make that joke for years. He clears his throat and continues, "Anyway, to Sid and Mary Ann. May they enjoy many happy years together."

I take a sip of my champagne as I look around the room. To my surprise, Suzie isn't drinking. She didn't drink any wine yesterday either claiming she was the designated driver. I raise an eyebrow at her and she blushes. Suzie blushing? There's only one reason the crazy woman would blush. She's totally pregnant. I wink in response.

"Why are you winking at Suzie?" Hailey asks.

I run a finger over my throat, but she either doesn't get I'm trying to signal her to shut it or she doesn't care. With this group, it could go either way.

Hailey's eyes move to Suzie and widen when they see she's holding apple juice. "You're pregnant!" she shouts, loud enough for the entire state to hear.

Suzie shushes her. "It's Sid and Mary Ann's big day. I don't want to take the spotlight away from them."

"Oh, this is exciting," Mary Ann says. "Does this mean I get to be an aunt?"

While the men pat Grayson on the back, the girls gather around Suzie. "I really am sorry to ruin your day," she apologizes to Mary Ann.

"It's fine. This isn't my first rodeo either." She waves away Suzie's concerns. "Besides, you're adding to the happiness."

"Shall we have some cake?" Max announces. He motions to someone behind him who wheels in a tray carrying a three-tier wedding cake.

When I get a closer peek, I realize the wedding topper is a dominatrix wearing leather and chains. She's holding a whip and lashing the groom. I glare at Max. I can't believe he and his brothers pulled a prank on Sid's wedding day!

The cart rolls to a stop in front of the couple. Sid looks down and sputters.

Mary Ann giggles before asking in a loud voice, "How did they know?"

Sid growls at his bride. "We are not into BDSM and we both know who's in charge in the bedroom."

"Ahem," I clear my voice loud enough to catch their attention. "Little ears."

"My ears are not little," Suzie exclaims.

Ollie elbows her. "She's talking about me, doofus."

Sid glares at his brothers. "I'll get you back for this."

They all look around and whistle like they have no clue what he's talking about. As if. Max presents the couple with a cake knife and Mary Ann cuts a perfect triangle piece of cake. My mouth waters when I see it's chocolate cake with a thick layer of buttercream frosting. Yum.

I watch as Sid feeds Mary Ann a sliver of cake. She licks her lips and winks at him as she swallows. "My turn," she says and picks up the entire piece she cut and smashes it into his face. Then, she squeals like a little girl and rushes off with Sid chasing her.

"I think I'm going to like Aunt Mary Ann," Suzie declares.

"We might as well eat," Max says and motions everyone to the large table set up in the middle of the room. "We won't be seeing them for a while."

I take my seat next to Max with Ollie on the other side of me. As I look around the table of the mismatched family teasing each other, I think I can get used to this. The thought practically scares the pants right off of me. Good thing I'm wearing a skirt today.

Chapter 27

If the day doesn't end with someone crying, did you really have a family day?

I'M LAYING ON THE sofa in my pajamas when someone knocks on the door Sunday morning. I groan and scoot further under my blanket. Maybe if I stick my head under it, I can pretend there's no one at the door. I am in no way prepared for visitors. I haven't combed my hair yet, let alone prepared breakfast for Ollie. Apparently, Ollie doesn't need any breakfast to be full of energy since he jumps to his feet and rushes to the door.

"Tell whoever it is, I moved to Timbuktu," I shout at his back.

Max walks into the apartment and shuts the door behind him. "I wouldn't recommend a move to Timbuktu since there's a war going on there and all."

"It's a figure of speech." I try to stand and get tripped up in my blanket. I start to fall but Max catches me before my face meets the floor. "What are you doing here?" I ask once I manage to untangle myself from the blanket.

"I thought I'd take you and Ollie on an excursion today."

Ollie whoops. "Awesome. I'll get dressed." He runs off without a backward glance.

I stare after him. "I haven't seen him excited to get ready to go somewhere in at least a year."

"The teenage years are tough," Max says before grasping my chin and tilting my head back. "Good morning, sweetheart," he whispers when his mouth is a breath away from mine. His lips meet mine, and I sigh as his sweet and spicy taste hits me. His hand moves away from my chin to wrap around my waist and draw me near but not near enough. I rise on my toes and thread my hands through his hair.

"Ugh. Gross. Not in front of the kid."

We break apart, and I look over to see my son whirling toward the hallway with his hand over his eyes. He runs straight into the wall. "Ouch! Who put this wall here?"

I shake my head and return my attention to the delicious man in front of me. "I guess I better get dressed since we're apparently going out today."

"Have you eaten breakfast yet?" he asks and lifts a paper bag.

"Ooh. What did you bring?" I try to peek in the bag, but he swats my hand. "Go get showered and dressed."

When I come out of the bathroom after my shower, I can smell bacon. My stomach rumbles, and I rush through dressing. If Ollie gets his hands on the bacon, there won't be any left for me. I throw on a pair of jeans and a sweater and speed walk to the kitchen. My eyes nearly pop out of my head at the sight greeting me.

"Where did all this food come from?" I ask as I study the kitchen counter covered in bacon, eggs, pancakes, and French toast.

"Pops made it," Ollie says and grins to show me the partially chewed pancake in his mouth.

I say the words, "Don't talk with food in your mouth," without thinking and then turn to Max. "You made all of this?" He nods. "I didn't know you could cook."

"Who do you think helps out when Carol's sick?" Carol is the chef at the pub. She makes the best tuna melt I've ever eaten.

My stomach rumbles again, and Max picks up a plate. "Have a seat. Do you want maple syrup or honey on your pancakes and French toast?"

"Um…" I'm too dazed by a man cooking in my kitchen to answer. The only reason Silas ever went into our kitchen was to get a beer out of the refrigerator. I don't think he knows how a stove works, let alone how to actually use one.

Max chuckles at my obvious dazzlement. "I'll get you both." He places a plate piled high with food and a cup of coffee in front of me. He kisses my hair before sitting across the table from me. This is everything I wanted when I married Silas. Lazy Sunday mornings around a kitchen table before going on an adventure.

Speaking of adventures, "What did you have in mind for today?"

"The local animal shelter is holding a fundraiser. Considering the kid made me foster kittens, I figured he'd want to help out."

"Cool. Do we like clean out the cages or what?"

Max ruffles his hair. "No cleaning duties today. They have a few games set up to help raise money."

As we finish our breakfast, Max tells us all about the no-kill shelter the fundraising is benefitting. "You know a lot about this place," I say as we pick up the dishes.

"I donate a gift certificate for the pub each year."

I lift up on my toes to kiss his cheek. "You're a sweet man, Max McGraw."

The dishes finished, we pile into Max's truck and head to the park where the fundraiser is happening.

"Do you think they'll have dogs you can adopt there?" Ollie asks as we drive, and I groan.

"Ollie—"

Max pats my thigh. "They will, but you can't get a dog when you live in an apartment. A dog needs space to run."

Ollie huffs but drops the issue. I mouth *thank you* at Max, and he winks in return. His wink should be classified as a lethal weapon because my heart nearly explodes when it's directed my way.

We arrive at the park, and I'm happy to see there's a decent crowd gathered. Max takes my hand as we walk. I watch for Ollie's reaction, but he's not paying us any attention. No, his eyes are riveted on the puppies in the cage. I feel a repeat of the no puppy conversation coming on.

"Go on," Max says. "You can play with them but don't fall in love. You can't bring one home."

Ollie shakes his head. "Maybe it's better I don't play with them then."

I sigh, and Ollie rolls his eyes. "She's got the mushy look on her face again."

"I can't help it. When you act all grown-up and make me proud, this is how I react."

"Whatever," he grunts, but I see the smile on his face before he looks away.

"Who wants to throw darts at balloons?" Max asks.

"I bet I can hit more balloons than you," Ollie challenges.

"You're on."

Fifteen minutes later, the charity has raised fifty dollars from us, and Ollie is waving his winnings in Max's face. They're merely drink coupons, but you'd think he'd won a million dollars with the way his chest puffs up.

"Drinks on me," he yells and rushes off to one of the vendors.

"Get me a hot chocolate!"

He flicks his fingers in a two-fingered wave I've seen Max and his friends do a million times. I'm not sure if I should be happy he has adult males to hang around with or annoyed their alpha male ways are rubbing off on him.

"You didn't have to let him win," I tell Max.

He shrugs. "No skin off my back."

After Ollie returns with our drinks, we play count the dog biscuits and pick an egg before moving on to bingo.

"Think you can handle losing to me again, old man," Ollie teases.

Max wraps an arm around his neck and messes with his hair. "Not the hair!" Ollie complains as he pushes Max off of him.

Max rubs his hands together. "I feel a winning streak coming on. How many cards does everyone want?"

"I can pay for our cards."

Max's eyes clearly communicate how stupid he thinks me paying is. I grunt and tell him five. He pays for the cards, and we find an empty table.

"It's going well, don't you think?" Max whispers to me while Ollie is engrossed in the game.

"Are you trying to win my son over?" I tease.

"Of course, I am. I know you're a package deal."

Darn it. I must have drank my hot cocoa too quickly and it caused heartburn because it can't be my heart melting at his words.

"Ma," Ollie hisses. "Pay attention. You missed one." He stamps a number on my card, and I return my attention to the game.

"Oh my," I say when I look down. "Bingo."

"That's not how you do it," Ollie criticizes before yelling, "Bingo!" at the top of his voice.

Max stands and takes my card. "I'll get your prize for you." He kisses the top of my head before sauntering off.

"I like Pops," Ollie tells me as soon as Max is out of hearing range.

"I thought you didn't like him," I say because he might be acting like best buds with him now, but he really didn't like the man a short time ago.

"He grew on me." He shrugs. "Anyway, you should probably tie him down before another woman does."

"Tie him down? What is he? A steer?"

He bumps my shoulder. "You know what I mean."

"Spell it out for me." I don't want to make assumptions when the subject is this important.

"I mean I approve. I wouldn't mind having Pops as a stepdad. And Hailey's a pretty cool stepsister, too."

My mouth drops open, and I lose the ability to speak for a minute as I fantasize about Max being my husband. Falling asleep every night safe in his arms. Waking up every morning cuddled up next to him in bed. No, I shake my head. His life is here in the city. Mine is in a city three-hundred and fifty-some miles away. This is all temporary.

"I think you're getting carried away," I manage to say when the ability to speak returns to me.

"Don't be an idiot, Ma," he says and walks away to see what prize I've won.

I stare after him, but my legs refuse to move. Is Ollie right? Am I being an idiot for holding back from Max? No, I'm not holding back. I'm being cautious and taking it slow. Slow and steady wins the race. If only I could believe my own words.

Chapter 28

Every time I feel like quitting, I remember there's a child somewhere whose relentless persistence paid off and resulted in a bedtime three hours later than usual.

I'M FILLING IN FOR Suzie at *You Cheat, We Eat* on Monday since morning sickness hit her hard today. I'm excited our group will soon be joined by one tiny baby. Wait. When did I start considering myself part of the group of Max's friends and family? We might not even be in Milwaukee when the baby is born six months from now. My heart squeezes at the thought of missing the birth of Suzie and Grayson's child. Dang it. Max and his friends and family are reeling me in, and I am apparently powerless to resist.

I jump up from my place behind the reception desk. I'm supposed to be working. This is not the time to wallow in thoughts of what I'll be missing out on if we return to Saint Louis. No, not if. When.

Since Hailey and Phoebe are out on a job, I've been tasked with making sure Lola and Leroy get some exercise this morning. Now is the perfect time to get off my rear and take a walk. I peek my head into Phoebe's office where Ryker is working.

"I'm going to walk the dogs and get a coffee. You want one?"

"Black," he says and takes out his wallet.

"I got it." He grunts again, and my lips purse. I leave before I'm tempted to give him a mom lecture on proper speaking etiquette.

I walk toward the small dog park a few blocks away muttering to myself about Max, the future, Suzie's baby, and the hodgepodge group of people who call themselves a family. *Stop it! No more worrying about the future and whether Max has a place in it. You have enough to worry about.*

When a passerby jumps out of my way, I realize I must be talking out loud. Great. Now I look like the crazy woman who talks to herself. This is what I get for hanging around Suzie. The woman personifies crazy. I force myself to look up and smile at the other pedestrians. Guessing by the cringes, I'm not looking like any less of a crazy woman. I let my smile drop and speed up my steps. The dogs take this as a cue to run.

"Whoa!" I command as if they're horses and not dogs. They bark in excitement, and I tighten my grip on their leashes.

By the time I return to the office half an hour later, my mind is calmer, but my hair is a mess, and my clothes are mud-stained. Lola and Leroy might be well-behaved, but the same can't be said for the other dogs in the park who thought jumping on me was the best idea ever. Their owners got a dose of Bossy Mom, that's for sure.

I lay Ryker's coffee on his desk. He looks up and smirks. "Oh, shut it, big guy."

His smirk changes to a smile as he chuckles. He points to my head. "You have a leaf in your hair."

"Of course, I do!" I stomp off to the bathroom.

Hailey and Phoebe return an hour later with fresh coffees. "Bless you," I say as Hailey hands me a mocha latte.

"You're welcome." At the sound of Hailey's voice, the dogs that had been sleeping on their beds in her office, bark and come barreling out of her office. Leroy heads straight to Hailey, but Lola aims for Phoebe.

"No. Down," Phoebe squeals as Lola climbs her like a tree and starts humping away. She closes her eyes and her nose wrinkles as she tries to shove Lola off of her. Her fighting only seems to spur Lola on more.

"Does Leroy not take care of Lola?" I ask between bouts of laughter.

Hailey frowns and grabs Lola's collar. "Stop, Lola. Phoebe isn't a big juicy steak."

"Steak? Don't encourage her. She'll try and eat me."

A chair squeaks before heavy footfalls approach. "Lola. Down," Ryker commands.

Lola whimpers and drops to her hind legs. She looks up at Phoebe with those big brown puppy dog eyes. I wouldn't be surprised if she licked her lips.

"At least you're not in your Loubobo shoes. Lola would have had you on the ground in two seconds flat if you were wearing those ridiculous heels." Hailey whistles and Lola walks to her with her hand hanging down.

Phoebe shudders. "It's Louboutins." Hailey winks at me and mouths *I know.*

"Come on, Princess. Let's get you cleaned up." Ryker tags her hand and leads her to the restroom.

"You might want earphones for what happens next," Hailey tells me.

"We're not having sex in the restroom," Phoebe shouts.

"Yeah, sure," Hailey shouts back but mouths to me *they totally are.*

"Stop it." I hear Phoebe gasp. "I'm not having sex with you in here while Hailey and Faith listen." Her long moan tells a different story.

I jump up from my chair. "Why don't I go get lunch?"

Before I can make it to the door, it bangs open and a woman stomps in. Judging by the red face and pinched nose, she is not a happy camper.

"I demand to speak to someone this instant!"

I force a smile on my face. "Welcome to *You Cheat, We Eat.* How may we help you?" I motion to a chair, but she shakes her head and starts pacing the room.

"I can't believe this," she mutters.

"What can't you believe, Ms. ...?" Hailey asks.

"It's Mrs. Wagner, which you should know since I hired you." She points her finger at Hailey. "And you've done nothing!"

I walk backwards until I'm behind the desk and take a seat. I keep one eye on the irate woman while I search the files. Sure enough. Mrs. Wagner is a client. I retrieve the file and skim it while Hailey reads over my shoulder.

"I'm sorry, Mrs. Wagner, but I don't understand what the problem is," Hailey begins. The woman sputters but Hailey continues. "I followed your husband for two weeks at various times of the day and night. I found no evidence he's cheating on you."

"But he is cheating on me! I know it! I just need the proof and then I can divorce his ass."

Hailey motions behind her. "Would you like to talk further in my office?"

"No! I don't need to talk in your office. I want you to find evidence my husband is cheating."

Behind Mrs. Wagner, the restroom door opens, and Phoebe and Ryker step out. Mrs. Wagner doesn't notice as Ryker pushes Phoebe into their office and stands guard in front of the door.

"What makes you think he's cheating?" Hailey asks in a calm voice.

"He's working all kinds of hours and doesn't pay any attention to me."

Hailey consults the file. "From the surveillance I performed, your husband was home by seven each night." She taps the computer screen. I skim the lines she's pointing at. My eyes widen as I read how Mr. Wagner came home to a dark house on several occasions.

"I do not accept your findings!"

Hailey opens her arms wide. "You're free to hire another private investigator. I can give you a list of names, but I think they'll tell you the same thing I have – there is no evidence your husband is having an affair."

Mrs. Wagner stomps her foot. "I don't want to hire another investigator. I want you to do the job I hired you for. Find proof my husband is cheating."

"I'm sorry, Mrs. Wagner, but I don't fabricate lies."

The woman raises her arm as if to slap Hailey. Hailey doesn't move. She stares at her as if daring Mrs. Wagner to go ahead. The door opens behind her and a woman walks in. Her eyes scan the room before she moves forward and takes Mrs. Wagner's arm. She makes some quick move and suddenly Mrs. Wagner's arm is pinned to her back and she's being frog-marched out of the office.

"I think you're done here," the stranger says as she opens the door with her free hand. She leaves the door open, and Hailey and I rush behind her to watch as she marches the *former* client to the elevator and pushes her inside.

"I advise you calm down before returning," the stranger says as the doors close. She waits until the elevator reaches the ground floor before returning to our office.

I study the woman as she walks toward us. She's tall, a good inch or two taller than Hailey who's already tall for a woman at five-foot-eight. She's skinny, but unlike me, she has the curves of a woman. Her long blonde hair is pulled into a low ponytail. Her light blue eyes are currently twinkling in humor. Guessing by the laugh lines around her eyes, she's about my age.

Hailey puts her hands together like she's praying and bats her eyelashes. "Please tell me you're here to apply for the office manager job."

"I'm here to apply for the job."

"You're hired!"

I nudge Hailey with my hip. "Maybe you want to ask her name first?"

"Christina Lindberg. Everyone calls me Chrissie."

"I'm Hailey Barnes." They shake hands, but Hailey refuses to let her go. She uses her hand to drag Chrissie further into the office.

"I'm Faith. I'm filling in."

"She's also my dad's girlfriend," Hailey explains, and I elbow her.

"She doesn't need to know my relationship status," I hiss.

Hailey shrugs. "We're all one big family here. If she can't handle personal information about us, she probably shouldn't work here."

Lola and Leroy rush out of Hailey's office to greet the visitor. Lola jumps up, and Chrissie yells, "Heel!"

The dog drops to her hind legs and whimpers before skulking back to the office with her tail between her legs. Leroy follows her.

Phoebe's mouth drops open. "She's like the dog whisperer." Then, she whirls around to confront Ryker. "Why didn't you do anything when Mrs. Wagner was about to hit Hailey?"

"Hailey had things under control."

Hailey beams a smile his way. "I sure did."

Phoebe grunts but walks forward to introduce herself to Chrissie. "I'm Phoebe." She points to Ryker. "He's Ryker, my husband."

Chrissie shakes hands with Phoebe and Ryker before addressing Hailey, "Do I interview with all of you at the same time?"

Hailey snorts. "Interview? You're hired." She motions to her office. "Come on in and we can discuss details."

As soon as they disappear into the office, Phoebe rushes to the door and places her ear on it.

"What are you doing?"

"Shush. I can't hear anything."

I shake my head before returning to my desk. I hum to myself as I get back to work. I'm going to miss these guys if I return to Saint Louis. This time, I don't correct my 'if' to 'when'. There's no sense lying to myself after all.

Chapter 29

I try to maintain a positive attitude. My record is one minute and twenty-seven seconds.

"You ready for a break?" Max asks me the next morning as he walks into the pub where I'm cleaning.

I glance around the room. "I'm nearly done. There's no sense stopping until I'm finished."

Max looks at the clock and cringes. "I'm sorry. I didn't realize how late it was. I've been dealing with a problem with a distributor."

My heart unclenches. It's been clenched with worry since our usual coffee break time came and went, and I didn't hear a peep from Max. Stop acting like a hormonal teenager, I berate it.

"Why don't we have lunch, then, before the pub opens?" Max offers.

Before I can respond, my phone rings. "Sorry," I say as I fish it out of my pocket. My heart picks up when I see who's calling. "Agent Judson."

"Do you have a minute?" he asks without bothering with small talk. Judson always has time for small talk. Is this the call I've been waiting for?

I nod and then realize he can't see me. "Yes," I say as I find a chair and collapse into it. Max sits next to me and takes my free hand. He squeezes as if to reassure me I'm not alone.

"I've got good news for you." My heart stops, and I forget to breathe.

Max's hand massages circles on my back. "Breathe for me, sweetheart."

I force air back into my lungs. "Tell me," I insist into the phone.

"You can come home."

"What? How? When?"

Judson chuckles. "Police responded to an anonymous call at a house the gang frequents. The place was filled to the rim with drugs and weapons. Everyone in the house was arrested. They won't be breathing free air for a long time. Trust me, by the time they do get out, they'll have forgotten all about Ollie."

None of his words make sense. Of course, the gang has drugs and weapons. The question is how they usually manage to run roughshod on the city. But I don't bother asking questions or demanding an explanation. I'm more interested in the end result.

"We can really come home, then?"

"Yeah, Faith. You and Ollie can come home." I hear a siren in the background. "Crap. I need to go. Call me if you have any questions."

I hang up without saying good-bye. Max takes the phone from my shaking hands. He stands and hauls me to my feet before pulling me into his arms and twirling me around. "I'm happy for you, sweetheart."

At his words, the news finally breaks through my foggy brain. I'm safe. I can go home. Except I feel like I'm home right here right now with Max's arms around me holding me close. Ah, shit. I went and did it, didn't I? I fell for Max despite telling my heart not to go there. Stupid heart. It never listens to me.

I tap his shoulder. "I need a minute."

His brow wrinkles, but he doesn't hesitate to set me down. "Are you okay?"

I don't respond. I can't. I've lost the ability to speak. I squeak and flee to the restrooms. Since no one else is here yet, I don't hesitate to lock the door behind me before sinking to the floor. I bury my face in my hands as my heart beats out of control.

What am I going to do? My life is in Saint Louis, not here. My heart – the stupid organ that refuses to listen to reason – reminds me Max is willing to sell the pub and move to Saint Louis with me. I can't allow him to leave his family, can I? What kind of woman would I be? Besides, I don't want to leave his family.

Not now, I tell myself. Now is not the time to worry about moving and family. I'm not going to solve the problem sitting on the floor in the restroom anyway. First things first. Telling Max I love him. What am I thinking? I can't tell him I love him now. It will sound contrived after the news I just received. No, I need to think of a special way to tell him. Or maybe show him? I shake my head. These are thoughts for another day. For now,

I need to put on my happy face and go outside and celebrate with Max.

Except when I walk into the pub, it's no longer empty. Max's brothers have arrived. My feet come to a halt before I can enter the bar area. I slap my forehead. Of course! His brothers are the ones who took care of my problem. It has to be. I've been here for months, but a few short weeks after Max and his brothers learn everything about my past, my problems are miraculously resolved?

I straighten my shoulders and march into the room. "Which one of you is responsible for solving my problems?"

They each look briefly my way before turning away and starting to whistle, but I notice the upturn of Wally's lips. I launch myself at him.

"Thank you!" I kiss his forehead.

Max yanks me away. "Hey now. You can show your appreciation in another way. No need to get your lips anywhere close to my brother."

I slap his shoulder. "Stop acting like a caveman. It's not like Wally is going to get ideas from me kissing his forehead."

Wally puffs up his chest. "I don't know. I am the better looking of the two of us."

Although I disagree – Max is literally the hottest man I've ever met – Wally isn't completely unfortunate looking. I know he's a few years older than Max, but you can't tell by looking at him. Sure, he's uptight, but he can still turn a woman's head. He's tall and, judging by the size of his shoulders and biceps, he's hiding a fit body underneath his clothes. His black hair doesn't have a hint of gray in it, but there is some gray in his beard. The uptightness ends when you look into his dark, green eyes. When those eyes study me, I could swear he can read every secret I have.

"What about me?" Sid asks and flexes his bicep.

"What are you doing here?" I ask and his face falls. "You got married Saturday, numbskull. Shouldn't you be on a honeymoon somewhere?"

He smirks. "Don't worry. Mary Ann is being treated right."

I cross my arms over my chest. "Treated right means laying on a beach somewhere sipping fruity drinks out of a coconut."

"Mary Ann already used up her vacation days this year. I booked us a cruise for February."

I raise my hand and bump fists with him. "Good thinking. February up north is hell." I remember this past winter and shiver. I am not looking forward to the snow and sludge and cold wind whipping off the lake. Max wraps his arm around me and draws me close.

"Why did Frosty the snowman want a divorce?" Barney asks. As usual, he doesn't wait for anyone to guess an answer before he gives it to us. "Because he thought his wife was a flake."

He guffaws and raises his hand for a high-five. I stare at it. "Corny."

"How is sex like snow?"

Max growls. "Barney."

"You never know how many inches you're going to get or how long it's going to last."

"I told you no dirty jokes in front of Faith." Max releases me to go after Barney.

I grip his arm to stop him. "Hold up." I raise an eyebrow at Barney. "Do you not know how many millimeters you are or are you worried about your performance? Because I have a tape measure and there's a blue pill for the other problem."

Barney gasps. "Millimeters?"

I raise my eyebrow. "If the shoe doesn't fit."

Lenny ruffles my hair. "Look at you. Fitting right in with your man's friends. I feel like this is the beginning of a beautiful friendship."

His words cause warmth to course through my veins. Since my parents left Saint Louis and my marriage fell apart, Saint Louis hasn't felt like home. But I never wanted to admit that to myself. Not when my kid has his school and all his friends and activities there.

Max's arms tighten around my middle. Of course, I've never felt love like I feel here either. Love. What am I— No, I stop those thoughts in their tracks. I am not going to ruin the celebratory lunch by worrying about the future. I can worry about the future tomorrow.

Chapter 30

What's my superpower? I'm a single mom. Isn't that enough?

I'M STARING AT MY phone the next evening trying to figure out how to tell Max I love him when it beeps with a message from Hailey. I startle and nearly fall off the sofa.

Girls Night Out. Now. Pub.

Before I have a chance to respond, my phone beeps again.

Bring Ollie. He can do his homework at Pop's place.

I glance over at Ollie who's sitting at the kitchen table working on his homework. What kind of mom am I if I force him to go somewhere else to do his homework because I want to have a good time? A rotten mom, that's what kind of mom I would be. The universe is not getting those points from me today!

I'm typing a message telling them I'm passing tonight when the doorbell rings. Ollie jumps up and races to the door.

"Hi, Suzie," he greets when he opens the door.

"Hey, little brother," she says.

Ollie laughs. "I'm like half a foot taller than you."

"What are you doing here?" I ask before they can get out the measuring tape.

"I'm your designated driver. I'm at your service for the next five and a half months." She does a bow but loses her balance. Ollie has to grab her arm to steady her before she does a nosedive.

"You're not planning to breastfeed then?"

She pales but ignores my question. "I knew you wouldn't show up at the pub if someone didn't come and drag your ass out."

"Language."

Ollie rolls his eyes. "I hear much worse at school, Ma."

I ignore him. "I think I'll stay in tonight," I tell her.

"Is this because you think you'll be a crap mom if you go out once in a while?"

My lips purse. How dare she know what I'm thinking? "I'm not going to drag Ollie across town, so I can have a night out."

Ollie bounces on his toes. "I get to go to the bar with you? Cool."

"Sorry, kid. You're relegated to Pops' apartment to do your homework," Suzie explains.

"Awesome!" He rushes off to gather his books.

I glare at Suzie. "You're diabolical."

She does an evil laugh while drumming her fingers together. "I'm practicing to be a mom and taking lessons from the best mom I know."

I roll my eyes. "You don't have to butter me up. I can't say no now anyway."

We walk into the pub thirty minutes later. Max grins when he sees us. "Hey, sweetheart." He kisses my cheek before greeting Ollie with some complicated handshake. When did they develop their own handshake?

"Your girls are over there." He points to a booth where Suzie has already joined Phoebe and Hailey. "I'll take him upstairs." I bite my lip. I feel like I'm abandoning my kid. "I got this." Max shoves me toward the group.

"Behave," I warn Ollie.

"What am I gonna do, Ma? Run away to the circus?"

"No circus, kid," Wally says as he walks in. "Circuses have clowns."

I giggle at how freaked out he looks at the idea of clowns. There's a story there.

"Get your skinny butt over here," Suzie calls from the other side of the bar. "I want to inhale the smell of your drink."

Max squeezes my hand. "He'll be fine. And he'll be a staircase away."

"I'm not a baby, Ma."

"Fine. Get out of here," I tell him and walk away before I can change my mind.

As I settle myself at the booth, a waitress arrives and sets a glass of red wine on the table. "Orders from the boss. Keep the pretty lady supplied with wine and food."

"How come she gets better service than we do?" Suzie asks.

Hailey giggles. "Because she's giving it to him," she says, and my face heats with a blush.

Phoebe groans. "You promised not to talk about Pops and Faith being intimate."

Suzie snorts. "Being intimate? Is that what the kids are calling it these days?"

"Why don't I bring you guys a platter of nachos?" The waitress says before escaping.

Hailey rubs her hands together and wiggles her eyebrows. "How do you think Sid's going to respond to the cake topper prank?"

"I think we're going to find out real soon." Suzie points to Sid who's now standing at the entry to the hallway leading to Max's apartment.

I frown. "My kid better not get injured."

Suzie waves away my concern. "Yeah, yeah. It's all fun and games until someone gets their eye poked out."

I hear a shout and a bunch of swear words before Max comes barreling into the bar. His hands are batting away at his head. He yanks something out of his hair and throws it at Sid. "Not funny, dude. What if Ollie had come back down before me?"

Sid pales as his eyes find mine. "Sorry, Faith. I didn't think."

I want to be angry, but this prank seems pretty harmless. "I get it. Men and thinking don't exactly belong together."

"In my defense, I set up the spider trap before I knew you were bringing Ollie over."

I'm glad Ollie didn't walk into whatever a spider trap is. My son hates spiders with a vengeance. He's totally fine with snakes and other creepy crawlers that freak me out. But spiders? No way.

Max punches Sid's arm. "Assume Ollie or Faith are going to be here from now on."

Here from now on? My jaw drops open but before I can begin to fathom a response to his words, the door bangs open and Chrissie walks in. Happy for the distraction, I raise my hand to gain her attention, but Hailey yanks my arm down. "Wait. I want to see what happens."

Wally is the first to approach her. "Hey, beautiful. I haven't seen you around here before."

Chrissie throws her head back and laughs. "That's your pick-up line? You haven't seen me around here before?"

Lenny pushes Wally out of the way. "Hey, doll. I'm Lenny."

She raises an eyebrow at the hand he extends. "Nope. Lame. Next!"

Barney swaggers to the front of the group. "Do you believe in love at first sight? Or should I walk past you again?"

She laughs and raises a fist to bump his. She looks around the place and notices our group. She waves and walks away from the men without a backward glance. They follow her like a puppy on the trail of a good scent.

"Who's this?" Wally asks when Chrissie sits down at our booth.

"This is Chrissie. She's the new office manager at *You Cheat, We Eat.*"

In response to this news, Wally demands, "Last name."

She raises an eyebrow and stares at him. They stare at each other for a good minute, before she gives in. "Lindberg, Christina. Do you want my social security number as well?"

Wally smirks. "Don't need it."

"You'd be surprised," she says with a wink.

Suzie tilts her head back and cries, "Thank you, Goddess!"

"Why are you thanking the ceiling?" I ask.

"Now you're all loved up, things were bound to get boring around here." She throws her arm around Chrissie. "But Chrissie here is going to be a ton of fun."

Max approaches the table, and Chrissie rolls her eyes. "Not another one."

"This one's mine. Keep your paws off," I tell her.

Max's smile stretches from ear to ear. "You claiming me as your man?"

"Whatever," I mumble.

He holds his hand out to Chrissie. "I'm Max." He points to Hailey. "That one's my daughter." He points to Phoebe and Suzie. "Those two are my honorary daughters." They shake hands. "You can call me Pops."

"What does a woman have to do to get a drink around here, Pops?" she asks.

Suzie places her chin in her hands and bats her lashes at Chrissie. "I think I'm in love."

"Is she throwing us over for a new friend?" Phoebe asks Hailey.

Hailey shrugs. "No worries. She'll get bored of her shiny new toy soon enough."

Max takes my hand and hauls me out of the booth. "Excuse us, ladies."

Suzie grabs my free hand before I can get away. "She's ours tonight, Pops. Even our men aren't here tonight."

"We won't be long. Promise."

She frowns but allows Max to lead me away. He stops in the hallway. "I wanted to let you know Ollie's all settled in upstairs."

"You could have told me that in front of the girls."

"Yeah." He smirks. "But I couldn't have done this." His lips crash to mine, and I immediately open to him. I moan when his sweet and salty taste combined with a hint of whiskey hits my tongue. Whiskey has never tasted so good. He wraps his arm around my waist and drags me close until I'm plastered to him and I can feel exactly how excited he is.

"Ahem!" Suzie clears her throat.

Max stills for a moment before ending the kiss. He places his forehead against mine as we both gulp for air. "Later," he promises before squeezing my hip and stepping back.

Before I can manage to get my breath under control, Suzie is there taking my hand and dragging me away. "It's a good thing I came when I did. We wouldn't have seen you for hours otherwise."

I'm not understanding the problem.

Chapter 31

If my kid would just do what I ask and stop complaining about every single thing, I could be the mom I always wanted to be.

"Faith, Faith, Faith." Hailey shakes my arm as she sings my name. "Faith."

"Hailey. Hailey. Hailey. What? What? What?"

She folds her hands together and bats her eyelashes at me. "Can we take Ollie home with us?"

"It's a school night." I look at the clock. "And it's already after eleven." Great. I'm the worst mom ever. My kid is probably upstairs in Max's apartment hocked up on cookies and coke while I'm in the bar having a good time. Mom – Zero. Universe – Half a point. Since Ollie is undoubtedly deliriously happy, I'm knocking points off the universe's score.

Suzie slaps my arm. "Ow. What is your problem?"

She circles her face with her finger. "You've got the I suck at being a mom face on." When I only stare at her in response, she huffs. "What? Why does everyone think I'm stupid?"

Hailey wraps her arm around Suzie's shoulder and the two of them wobble for a minute until Chrissie steadies them. "I don't think you're stupid. I can't lie. I think you're a klutz. But stupid, you are not!" She raises her hand at the end and teeters forward. Chrissie grabs the back of her t-shirt and hauls her up.

"Are they always like this?" Chrissie asks me.

"No. Usually, Suzie is the troublemaker, but she's got a bun in the oven …"

She looks down at Suzie who's doing her best to keep a tipsy Hailey from tipping over. "She does look like a troublemaker."

"Who are you calling a troublemaker?" Wally's question booms next to my ear, and I squeak.

Chrissie smirks at him. "Jealous I'm not calling you a troublemaker? We both know I don't need to say the words for it to be true."

"Look, kid—"

She cuts him off. "I'm not a kid, and I'm definitely not your kid, so you can stop with the patronizing name and voice."

"This is going to be epic. Epic!" Suzie screams.

"What's going to be epic?" I'm sure Hailey thinks she's whispering but she's not. Not even close.

Ollie walks over to our group. "Hey, Ma. Is it okay if I go home with Hailey and Aiden?" He thumbs his finger toward Aiden who's waiting at the door.

"Hey, husband!" Hailey yells and waves to Aiden. "I'm hungry. Can we get tacos on the way home?"

"Cool! Tacos! See you tomorrow, Ma." Ollie tries to rush off, but I grab his hood to stop him.

"One, did I actually respond to your question about staying at Aiden and Hailey's tonight?"

His face darkens, and he shuffles his feet. "Um."

"Two, did you finish your homework?"

He rolls his eyes. "Yes. Geesh. Do you have to embarrass me in front of everyone?"

Aiden walks over and smacks him on the head. "Not cool, Ol. Your mom's only looking out for you."

Ollie ducks his head. "I'm sorry."

"Hey, Faith." Aiden greets me with a kiss on the cheek. "Sorry about the Ollie situation. I must have gotten my wires crossed. I thought you already agreed he could come home with us."

"Please, Ma. I have the first period off tomorrow anyway."

"Fine." Ollie whoops, and I cross my arms over my chest. He quiets down. "You will listen to Aiden and Hailey." Behind me, Hailey hiccups. "Maybe just Aiden. And not give them a hard time."

"Thanks, Ma." His smile is blinding. Maybe I'm not a lousy mom for sending my kid home with friends to give me a night with my boyfriend after all.

Aiden squeezes my shoulder. "Thanks, Faith. You can trust us."

"Tacos!" Hailey shouts and throws herself in Aiden's arms.

Aiden drags Hailey away with Ollie following behind them talking a mile a minute.

"Welp! I'm out of here. I guess no one needs my designated driver capabilities tonight after all." Phoebe left an hour ago when Ryker came and snatched her away after she drunk dialed him. Suzie raises an eyebrow at Chrissie. "Unless you want a ride?"

"Nah. I'm good, but I'll walk you to your car."

They both give me hugs and then leave. An arm snakes around my waist. "Are you okay with Ollie staying with Hailey?" Max asks.

I shrug. I don't know how I feel. He's fifteen. I don't need to watch over him every single second, but I haven't had anyone to help me watch over him in such a long time, I feel like I'm laying down on the job.

Max whirls me around. "There's nothing wrong with asking your family for help."

"I guess. It's just weird since I haven't had family in a long time."

It's been six years since my parents moved to Alaska. And I refuse to associate with Silas's parents. There's a limit to how many times a woman can be told she's doing everything wrong in raising her son. Like they did such a stellar job with Silas.

"Well," Max says and interrupts my musings about the parents, "you have family now." He kisses my hair. "You ready to go up?"

"Go up?" I feign a yawn. "It's getting late. I think it's time I head home."

"Is that how you're going to play it?" I widen my eyes and tilt my head like I'm completely innocent. "You asked for it."

He lifts me up and throws me over his shoulder. Cheers erupt in the bar. I pound on his back. "Let me down, you big oaf."

He ignores my struggles and carries me through the bar and up the stairs to his apartment. He doesn't slow down until he throws me on the bed. I bounce once before he lands on me.

"You've been driving me crazy all night," he growls before nipping my ear. He licks a path from my ear down my neck to my shoulder. I arch my neck to give him more space to maneuver.

"Me? Drive you crazy? Why whatever do you mean?" I tease but my voice is breathy and gives me away.

"Sending me hot looks across the room all night. Flipping your hair. Laughing with abandon." He sinks his teeth into the spot where my neck and shoulder meet. I gasp and my back bows off the bed. I rub my breasts against Max's chest, but there are way too many clothes in between us.

I reach for Max's flannel shirt and start unbuttoning it. My clumsy hands are entirely too slow. I grasp both sides of the shirt and yank it open as hard as I can. Buttons fly across the room.

Max chuckles. "In a hurry, sweetheart?" He stands and lets his shirt fall off his arms revealing his toned chest. I don't know when chests became such a turn-on, but his sure is. "Your turn."

I sit up and tug my sweater over my head. My bra is next, but Max is there pushing my hands out of the way. "I can take it from here."

I fall back on the bed. "Be my guest."

Except he doesn't immediately rip my bra off of me. No, those actions would be too easy for the big tease. Instead, he massages my breasts through the silk of my bra. My nipples harden, and he pinches them. I moan and arch my back in invitation. He doesn't take my invitation and continues to tease me by tracing the top edge of my bra with his index finger.

"Your skin is unbelievably soft here," he murmurs before dipping his head and replacing his finger with his tongue.

I rub my legs together to help alleviate the ache he's creating there. "You are cruel."

"And you love it," he claims.

"You're lucky I love you." I freeze. I didn't mean to say those words. Shit. Shit. Shit. This was not the plan. I sit up and my head connects with Max's. "Ow." I rub my forehead.

Max drags me up to the headboard and props me against it. "Are you hurt?" He tries to move my hand to look at my injury, but I smack him away. "Let me get you an icepack."

"I don't need an icepack. I need a second is all. Your head is freaking hard."

He leans against the headboard next to me and pulls me into his arms. "You sure you're not hurt?"

I lift my hand. "I don't even have a bump."

His fingers prod at my forehead until he grunts. "It doesn't look bad."

I roll my eyes. "Can we get back to our previously scheduled activities?" I ask hoping he'll forget the words I said.

"No way. You can't announce you love me and expect me not to respond."

"You're supposed to respond by making passionate love to me."

He winks. "Don't worry. We'll get to that portion of the night. First, I need to hear you say the words again."

I close my eyes and bury my head in his shoulder. "Why? Didn't you hear me the first time?"

He places a finger under my chin and lifts my head. "Sweetheart, I need to hear the words again."

"Fine! I love you. Are you happy now?"

His smile lights up his entire face. "Ecstatic." He seals his lips with mine for an all too brief kiss. I mewl when he lifts his head. "I guess it's time to put the pub up for sale, then."

My eyes widen and my jaw drops. "Just like that?"

"I love you. You love me. Your life isn't here. So, yeah. Just like that." His lips descend again, but I slap him.

"No, we need to talk about this. You can't decide to give up your entire life here on a whim."

He nibbles my ear. "Can't we talk about this later? I'm kind of busy here."

"You can be busy later," I insist, but then he licks a spot behind my ear, and I forget what I was saying. "Talk later. Lips now."

Max chuckles and proceeds to use his lips in all kinds of creative ways.

Chapter 32

Being a mom is basically yelling 'you just had a snack' over and over at your kid until you give in and throw him a snack.

It's Friday night, two days after I accidentally told Max I love him, and I'm doing my darndest to not freak out as I wait for him to arrive and take us out to dinner. Meanwhile, Ollie is bouncing in his seat with excitement. I'm glad he's looking forward to seeing Max since we have lots of news for him. News which is making my stomach clench.

"You sure you don't want to go out with your friends for Halloween?" I ask him.

"Ma," he whines. "I already told you I'm fine going out with you and Max."

I might have already asked him if he's sure a time or two. Fine, it was five times. I asked him five times. There's nothing wrong with a mom wanting to make sure her kid is happy.

The doorbell rings and Ollie shoots of his seat like a rocket. "Finally! I'm starving."

"It's five o'clock and you had a snack less than five minutes ago," I remind him.

Ollie ignores me to open the door. "Hey, Pops!"

Max ruffles his hair. "Hi, son. You ready for some pizza?"

"I'm starving," he repeats. "Ma wouldn't let me have a snack."

I clench my jaw before I can remind him – again – of the peanut butter and jelly sandwich he finished eating not five minutes ago. I know a losing battle when I see one.

Max walks over to me and takes my hands to draw me near. "Hi, Spitfire." He bends over and kisses my forehead.

Ollie feigns getting sick. "Not in front of the kid."

Max winks at me and motions to the door. "Shall we?"

You don't need to tell my kid twice. He's out the door and down the hallway before I can put my coat on. Max throws his arm around me and leads me out of the apartment. "Come on. We better catch up to the kid before he drives away."

Ugh. I groan. "Don't remind me. He has driver's education in January. I am not old enough to have a child who can drive."

He tickles my side. "And I am?"

I push his hands away and sprint for the stairs. "You're an old man. You can't keep up."

Of course, he can keep up. Max reaches his truck long before I arrive huffing and puffing like I ran a marathon instead of the three flights of stairs I ran down. He smirks at me, but I ignore him and climb into his truck.

We drive to the local pizza place. As I walk in, I'm assaulted by the sound of laughter and the smell of baking crust, melting cheese, and oregano. Yum. Ollie darts around me to an empty booth along the back wall.

"I guess we're sitting in the back," I tell Max. He takes my hand and leads the way.

Once we're seated and have ordered, the squirming begins. Max and I argued all night long on Wednesday about the future and what we should do. Well, not all night long. We had more vigorous activities to attend to. But in between *those* activities, we managed to have 'the talk'.

I tried in vain to change his mind about selling the pub. I don't want him to give up his life for me and end up regretting it. He told me the only thing he'd regret is not giving our relationship a chance. Of course, I melted at those words and gave in. His smooth-talking mouth does not bode well for me getting my way in the future.

Max insisted on being there when I tell Ollie about our relationship and the future. And insisted is putting it lightly. Since my son said he was fine with Max being his stepdad, I'm hoping this conversation will go smoothly. I can't help being nervous, though. Who wouldn't be in my situation?

Max squeezes my hand and dips his chin toward Ollie. It's time. I clear my throat. "Ollie, we need to talk to you."

"I figured. Go ahead."

"I got a call from Agent Judson this week," I start. Ollie's hands, which are tapping on the table, freeze. He doesn't know how often I've been in touch with Judson since the agent usually doesn't have any update besides to say, *hang in there.*

"Did something happen to the girl? Is she okay? They didn't get to her, did they?"

Of course, my son is worried about the victim of the attempted rape and not the possible danger to him. "She's fine. It's good news." I pause but he doesn't say anything. "We can go home. The gang members who were after you have been caught. They're going to be in prison for a long time."

"Cool." The waitress arrives with our drinks and some breadsticks. Ollie takes a breadstick and shoves it into his mouth.

"You don't have anything else to say?"

He shrugs. "I'm glad those kids are in prison."

Alrighty, then. On to the second topic on tonight's packed agenda. "There's more."

He swallows his breadstick before asking, "What else did Judson say?"

"No. Not Judson. About us. Max and I," I clarify.

He looks back and forth between the two of us. "Did he pop the question?"

I choke on my sip of wine and barely manage not to spray the entire table with it. Max chuckles as he rubs my back. "Not yet."

I slap his chest. Not yet? Does he not know kids don't understand ambiguous answers? "He didn't, but we love each other and—"

Ollie holds up his hand. "Yuck. Gross. I don't need the details."

Max laughs, and I slap him again. "Stop encouraging him."

"What? Sometimes us guys need to stick together." He bumps fists with Ollie.

I bury my face in my hands. What did I sign up for? Max grasps my forearms and forces me to look up or let my face fall to the table. "Come on, there's more to tell. Get it all out so we can enjoy our pizza when it comes."

I clear my throat. "Anyway, Max and I want to live together."

"Cool."

"Which means he'll be moving back to Saint Louis with us."

Ollie's nose wrinkles. "What? Why are we moving back to Saint Louis?"

"Because it's our home?" Wait. I didn't mean for my words to sound like a question. I try again. "Because Saint Louis is our home. Our friends and family are there."

"Grandma and Grandpa are in Alaska. And my friends are here."

I stare at him with my mouth hanging open. "What about your friends in Saint Louis?"

He shrugs. "We mostly lost touch. Besides, my school here is way cooler than the one there. Coach says I'll make varsity on the soccer team next year for sure. And there's a bunch of us trying to start up an environmental group. We're going to advise the school on how to lower its carbon footprint. Do you know they use all plastic utensils in the cafeteria? And they have tons of vending machines. All giving out items wrapped in plastic. There is no Planet B."

My mouth opens and closes, but I don't know what to say. I'm not an idiot. I've noticed how involved Ollie is with school activities here, but I didn't realize he wanted to stay in

Milwaukee. He never told me. Of course, I never asked either. I just assumed.

"Hailey loved the school, too. She taught drama there for a while."

Ollie's eyes widen. "Really? She'd be a cool teacher. Why'd she quit?"

"You'll have to ask Hailey. It's her story to tell."

"Hold on!" I place my hands on my head to stop the world from spinning. "Let me get this straight. You want to stay in Milwaukee?" Ollie nods. "What does this mean for us?" I ask Max.

"Easy. You and Ollie move into my apartment with me." Max says like it's the most obvious thing in the world.

"Awesome! Can I get a dog?" Ollie asks, and I groan.

"We'll see," I say automatically since I'm still stuck on the whole move in with Max thing.

He grunts. "We'll see means no," he tells Max.

"And sometimes," Max replies, "we'll see means we'll see."

"Ugh! Are you going to take Ma's side on everything?"

Good question. I look over at Max to see his reaction. He grins at me. "We'll see."

"When are we moving in?" Ollie asks as if everything is settled.

"Whoa! I haven't agreed to move into Max's place yet."

"Why not? He was going to live with us in Saint Louis. What's the difference if we live with him in Milwaukee?"

Damn kid. Always using reason and being logical.

"Oh. And I have a line on a job for you," Max moves on as if the entire matter of us moving into his apartment is settled.

"A job," I sputter. "I already have a job."

"But since it's safe for you to use your real name, I figured you'd want to get back to your paralegal work. One of the regulars at the pub mentioned he's looking for a legal secretary. I don't know if legal secretary and paralegal are the same thing, but I got his number in case you're interested."

"Good. Then you can stop bitching about your cleaning job."

"Language," I growl at Ollie. "I don't hate my cleaning job." He snorts.

Max tugs on a strand of my hair. "I get it. You don't need to be embarrassed. I know your opinion about cleaning has nothing to do with your opinion of my pub. Why do you think I asked my regular for his number?"

"Pizza's here," Ollie announces as the waitress arrives with two large pizzas fresh from the oven.

"We'll talk about this later," I tell Max.

He winks. "I'm sure we will."

Chapter 33

I love when my son tells me he's bored. As if the lady standing in front of a full sink of dirty dishes is the place to go for ideas about how to have a good time.

"MA!" OLLIE SCREAMS THE next morning. "Can you come in here?"

I groan. It's entirely too early for screaming. But, like the good mom, I like to think I am, I force myself to stand from the couch and walk to his room to see what his problem is now. When I open the door, my eyes nearly pop out of my head. His room is stuffed full of boxes. "Where did you get all these boxes?" No, wait. There's a more pressing question here. "What are you doing?"

"Duh, Ma. I'm packing."

"We're not moving into Max's until next weekend." Because I lost the argument there. To be honest, I don't know why I was fighting. I want to wake up to Max every morning and fall asleep in his arms every night. But the cautious part of me – the single mother in me – is telling me to slow things down. To be wary of who I bring into my kid's life.

The giddy high school part of me I didn't know existed until Max came along is telling cautious me to shove it. She reminds me Max has been a part of Ollie's life for months now. Hell, Ollie's the one who said he approved of Max before I brought the entire nerve-wracking subject of moving in with Max up.

"Can you help me move my desk? I dropped a book behind it, but I can't reach it."

I put my hands on my hips. "Let's talk about why you're packing first. Do you plan to live in a room filled with boxes?"

"Geez, Ma. It's for a week. Big deal. Besides, the sooner I get my room done, the sooner I can help you pack the rest of the house up."

I slump on his bed. Shit just got real. Am I ready to move in with a man? Will he turn into another Silas once the novelty of the relationship rubs off? Only Silas was never caring and romantic like Max.

"Stop being lazy, Ma. And help me."

I decide to have a freak out later when he's at his friend's house and I can have a proper freak out without spectators. I stand to help him move the desk. We've barely managed to pick it up when the doorbell rings and Ollie drops it. "I'll get it."

I manage to set my side of the desk down without it falling over and follow him to the front door. I'm surprised to see Hailey standing in the doorway. "Hey, Hailey. What are you doing here?" Oops. I sounded a bit snippy there. "Not that I'm not happy to see you."

Ollie bounces on his toes. "She's taking me out for the day."

Hailey wraps her arm around his shoulders. "I thought since he's my stepbrother now, we should take some time to get to know each other."

Stepbrother? When did someone switch the setting on my life to warp speed? I massage my temples to prevent the sudden headache I feel coming on. "It didn't take long for your dad to tell everyone, did it?"

She laughs. "Of course not. He's excited and in love."

Ollie places his hands over his ears. "Can we not talk about my mom being in love?"

Hailey plucks his hands away. "What? You not into girls yet? I thought you were fifteen."

He yanks his hands free of hers. "I'm into girls, but I don't want to hear anything about my mom's love life." He feigns gagging.

"Phoebe's the same way. She gets pale anytime we talk about Pops and your mom, which of course means we bring it up all the time."

"You're mean," Ollie accuses but there's a big smile on his face.

She shrugs but doesn't bother denying his accusation. "Anyway, what do you say? You want to hang with your stepsister today?"

"Can I, Ma?" He does the whole puppy dog eye thing. Every time I think I've grown immune to the look, I find myself falling for it once again.

"Are you going to cancel on your friend last minute? You hate when people cancel on you at the last minute." He's been excited about this Halloween get-together all week.

"It's no big deal. Andy's cool. He'll understand. Besides, he invited the entire class to the party. He won't notice I'm not there."

Of course, I give in. My kid has wanted a sibling forever. How can I deny him now? I can't. "All right. Let me grab my purse to get you some money."

Hailey stops me. "Today's on me." I don't bother arguing with her. The McGraws are too stubborn for me to deal with on a Saturday morning.

Once they leave, I collapse on the sofa. I should get up and start on the packing, but I'm exhausted. I can't skip a night of sleep anymore like when I was in my twenties or my thirties for that matter. Although Wednesday night was totally worth the exhaustion I'm feeling right now. Seriously. No regrets on my part there.

Besides, I can't blame my exhaustion completely on Wednesday night with Max. No, the topsy turvy turns my life took this week have to carry some of the blame as well. First, I'm moving back to Saint Louis with Ollie. Then, Max is coming with us. But in the end, it turns out we're staying here and moving in with Max. It's enough to give a person a migraine.

Someone knocks on the door. "What now?" I ask the room. "What now?" I repeat my question when the room doesn't provide me with an answer.

I stand but before I can reach the door it opens, and Max walks through carrying a load of collapsed boxes. Why did I let Ollie give Max his key? Rookie mistake.

"I guess I'm not getting today to work through all the changes in my life."

"Nope," he says and sets the boxes on the floor. "I'm not letting you change your mind about me or moving in with me."

I place my hands on my hips. "Did you convince Hailey to take Ollie out for the day, so we can pack the house without him in the way?"

His cheeks darken. "I might have mentioned something, but I didn't force her. You can't force my kid to do anything. She's excited about having a little brother."

"You know she's going to corrupt him."

He snorts. "I know she's going to try, but you're not going to let her."

"I guess I'll get dressed and we can get to work."

"Unless you need help in the shower. I'm an excellent back washer." He leers.

I shove him away. "If you join me, we won't get any packing done at all." Not a bad idea. I wiggle my eyebrows at him.

He places his hands on my shoulders and directs me toward the hallway. "Get moving."

I don't bother taking a shower. It'd be a waste of time since packing is dirty work. I throw on some jeans and an old t-shirt and pull my hair into a ponytail. When I return to the living room, Max is in the kitchen flipping pancakes.

"Right on time," he says when he notices me standing next to the counter. "Pour yourself a coffee."

"You don't have to cook for me, you know. I can cook." I don't know why I'm protesting. I'm loving having a man cook for me.

"Breakfast is my specialty," he says. "Since I was getting the pub up and running when Hailey was young, I wasn't around for dinner with my daughter. Instead, I always made sure to get out of bed and have breakfast with her before she went off to school."

My heart does a little skip. He's such a good dad. Max interprets my silence wrong. "Don't worry. The pub is an established business now. I don't need to be down there each and every evening. I'll make sure to have dinner with you and Ollie a few times a week."

"You misunderstand me," I tell him as I move close. "I was thinking about how awesome of a dad you are and how lucky my kid is to have you as a stepdad."

I push up on my toes to kiss him. I plan to touch my lips with his and step back, but when his taste combined with maple syrup hits me, I can't resist leaning in closer and lashing my tongue around his lips. He groans and drops the spatula to squeeze my neck. I moan and his tongue seeks entry.

Max uses his hand on my neck to twirl me around until my back is pushed up against the counter. His arm wraps around my waist and lifts me until I'm seated on the counter. I thread my hands through his hair and tilt my head for a better angle to enjoy his kiss. His thumb rubs circles in the back of my neck as he presses his lower body against me. I can feel his hardness at my belly.

Suddenly, Max yanks away from me and I nearly fall at the sudden loss of his support. "Sorry. Pancakes. Burning." He pants as he steadies me before reaching over to switch the burner off.

I look over his shoulder to see the pancakes are black. "Oops," I say and hop off the counter. "I guess you're going to have to eat something else for breakfast."

Heat ignites in his eyes. "You have anything particular in mind?"

"Maybe." I wink before spinning around and running toward my bedroom, giggling the entire way.

Max catches up to me in the hallway and throws me over his shoulder. He spanks my ass, but it doesn't hurt. "I think someone needs to be punished."

"Promises. Promises."

He throws me on the bed and crawls over me. "I always keep my promises."

Oh goodie.

Chapter 34

Whenever my teen cleans his room, I get a brand
new set of dishes.

I'M LAYING IN MY bed not sleeping the following Saturday
morning. It's not time to get up yet – it's still dark outside for
gosh sakes – but my mind is too busy flipping out to let my
body sleep. Am I doing the right thing? Cautious Faith has been
overthrown by in love Faith, and a woman in love is a woman
bound to make stupid mistakes. Trust me. I have the scars to
prove it.

There's a knock before the bedroom door opens and Ollie
walks in. I sit up. "What's wrong?"

"Nothing's wrong, Ma. Geesh." He flips on the light. Once
my eyes adjust to the sudden light, I notice he's holding a tray.

"What's going on?"

He comes closer and I see the tray is laden with breakfast food
– pancakes, bacon, eggs – and a mug of coffee.

"Since when do you know how to cook pancakes and bacon?"

"Pops taught me. We knew you'd be freaking out this morning, and we came up with the idea of me bringing you breakfast in bed."

I have no idea where to begin. When did they have time to hatch this plan? How come I haven't taught my boy to cook yet? Is this my future now? Max and Ollie teaming up against me? I let him place the tray over my lap as I work on recovering the ability to speak. "Thank you," is all I manage to come up with.

"You're welcome." He does a little bow. "Now, stop freaking out and eat your breakfast. Pops and my uncles will be here in an hour."

"Uncles?"

"Yeah. Wally, Sid, Lenny, and Barney."

"I know who you're talking about, silly. When did you start calling them your uncles?"

He shrugs and retreats before I can ask more questions. I take a sip of coffee before grabbing my phone off the bedside table and sending Max a message.

Thank you

He responds immediately despite it being way too early for him to be up on a Saturday morning after closing the bar down last night.

Anything for you, love.

Before I can set my phone down it lights up with another message.

Last morning of waking up to an empty bed. Looking forward to a lifetime of waking up to your beautiful face.

I melt at his words. Oh man, he's good at this romance stuff. I send him a smiling face with hearts emoji because I'm a total dork who's also in love.

By the time I finish my breakfast and get dressed, the sun is up, and Ollie is bouncing off the walls in excitement. I give him a rag and tell him to wipe down the shower. It doesn't need wiping down, but my kid needs to keep his hands busy before he hurts himself, or I give in to the temptation to tape him to a chair. The doorbell rings before he can walk away, and he throws the rag on the ground before running to the door like an excited kid instead of the surly teenager I've grown used to.

"Hey, son," Max says as he walks in. "You ready to move?"

"Did someone order muscles?" Barney asks as he walks in flexing his bicep.

Wally pushes him. "As if you have muscles."

"I've got muscles," Sid says as he walks in. He stops in front of me and strikes a pose.

Lenny pokes his finger at Sid's bicep. "You call that muscle?"

"Look, Ollie," I say. "The three stooges came over to help us move."

Lenny rubs a hand over his bald head. "Hey now. No making fun of the bald guy."

Max clears his throat. "Come on, wise guys. Let's get moving."

"Now, we're wise guys." Barney wrinkles his brow. "Are we the three stooges or wise guys?"

Max slaps him on the shoulder hard enough he has to take a step forward. Ollie giggles and Max winks at him.

"What's the deal with the furniture? You got room for it at your place?" Wally asks Max, but I answer.

"You can leave the furniture. I made an appointment with the thrift store to pick it up this afternoon."

Max takes my hand and drags me toward the hallway. "We'll be right back." He pulls me into my bedroom and shuts the door behind us. He presses me against the door and places his hands next to my head pinning me in place. "You don't have to give up your furniture. I can make room for it."

"I already gave up our furniture when we left Saint Louis. I didn't want to take the time to pack everything to bring it with us. The furniture out there is stuff I picked up in thrift stores. Trust me, I'm not sorry to see it go."

He places his hands on my cheeks and studies me. "You sure?"

"I'm sure."

He kisses my forehead. "Any other furniture you and Ollie want or need, you let me know and we'll make it happen."

I roll my eyes. "Stop spoiling me."

He kisses my nose. "Get used to it. I plan to spoil you for the rest of your life."

Someone knocks on the door. "You guys done in there? We're hungry," Barney whines.

Max closes his eyes and rests his forehead against mine. "One more day."

I kiss his cheek. "Thanks for checking on me. Let's get this done."

We walk into the living room hand in hand to discover the boxes from Ollie's room are already stacked at the front door. At this pace, we'll be done in no time.

Two hours later I'm unpacking kitchen stuff at Max's place. Although his kitchen has every utensil and gadget known to man, it's big enough to have plenty of space to add my stuff. At some point, I'll have to go through everything and decide what stays and what goes, but that's a chore for another day.

"Ma! Ma!" Ollie runs in clutching his nose.

"What happened?" I ask as I peel his hands away from his nose. Blood squirts out, and I snatch a kitchen towel from the box next to me. I tilt his head back and lead him to a chair in the dining area. Once he's seated with the towel containing the flow of blood, I ask again, "What happened?"

Ollie laughs and removes the towel with a flourish. "Gotcha!"

"Oliver Benjamin Bakker, what the hell did you do?"

"The guys showed me how to make fake blood with corn syrup and food coloring. Fooled you."

"You nearly gave me a heart attack, young man." I rub the spot on my chest where my heart rate is slowly returning to normal after the fright he gave me.

"Sorry, Ma."

I hear laughter and look over to see Max's friends are clutching their stomachs in amusement. They think this is funny, do they? I march over to them. "You think it's funny to fool a mom into thinking her kid is injured and scare her half to death?"

The laughter dies and none of them will look at me any longer. I cross my arms over my chest and glare at their bowed heads. "What would your mothers have to say about this?"

When no one answers, I continue to push. "Do you need me to call your moms and ask them?"

"I have the phone numbers for you," Max says as he joins me.

"We were only goofing around," Barney says.

Max growls next to me, but Barney speaks before he gets the chance. "We're sorry, Mama Bear."

The other three murmur their apologies.

"Not again, you hear?"

Ollie tugs on my hand. "I'm sorry, too. I messed up."

I squeeze his hand. "There's nothing wrong with messing up as long as you own up to it and learn from your mistakes," I tell him.

He rolls his eyes and tells the group of men. "I told you she turns everything into a teaching moment."

Max whistles. "All right. Break's over. Let's finish unloading the truck and then I'll order pizza."

His friends salute him before marching off to get more boxes from the truck. I start to walk back to the kitchen, but Max grasps my wrist and stops me.

"I have a surprise for Ollie."

Ollie whoops and jumps up and down. "What is it?"

"Now, son, before I give you this surprise, I'm thinking I need to apologize to your mom."

Apologize? There's only one reason he'd need to apologize. I yank my hand away from him. "Crap. You got him a dog, didn't you?" I blurt out before I can think better of it.

"A dog!" I have to cover my ears from Ollie's high-pitched scream.

I poke Max in the chest. "You agreed with me. You said an apartment was no place for a dog."

He captures my hand and holds it against his chest where I can feel his heart thumping away. "There's a small yard at the back of the building where we can let him out and a roof terrace he can run around on. Plus, there's a dog park two blocks away."

"But Ollie is way too busy to take care of a puppy."

"Ma, I'm not too busy. I'll take care of him. I promise."

There's no way I can deny him a puppy since Max dangled one in front of his face. I take a deep breath and shove my anger into a box I'll be opening when Max and I are alone tonight. "You're in trouble," I tell him.

He grins. "I'll make it up to you."

"You better. Now, go get this puppy."

He kisses me before walking to the landing. He returns holding a box with a ribbon on it. He hands the box to Ollie. "Welcome to the family, son."

Good grief. How am I supposed to stay mad at him when he says such sweet things to my son?

Ollie opens the box and picks up the most adorable puppy ever. His brown, fluffy fur makes him look like a baby bear and not a dog. "What's his name?"

"It's up to you to choose *her* name."

"It's a girl dog?" Ollie lifts her up to check. "Oh."

I kneel down next to him to pet the puppy. The fur is as soft as it looks. "What kind of dog is she?"

"She's a Labrador retriever. She was the runt of the litter."

Ollie holds her up next to his face. "Who are you calling the runt of the litter?"

"What are you going to name her?"

Ollie holds the squirming puppy in his hands and lifts her up to his face. "What do you think, girl? What's your name?" The puppy tilts her little head as she stares at Ollie before her pink tongue peeks out and licks his face. He giggles, and darn it, my heart melts, and right then I fall in love with the little furball. "Pepper."

"I think you should take Pepper for a tinkle before giving her a tour of her new home."

"Cool!" He removes a leash and collar from the box. He struggles to put the pink leash on the puppy who thinks he's playing a game, but he eventually manages. "Come on, Pepper. Walk time."

Once he leaves, I turn on Max. "I can't believe you!"

"The kid wanted a puppy."

"And you want him to like you," I accuse.

He takes my hand and pulls me into his lap on the sofa so I'm straddling him. He places a hand on my cheek. "I don't want him to like me. I want him to love me."

I melt, but then remember I can't give up too easily. I need to set a precedent for the future. I smack his shoulder. "Stop cheating!"

He chuckles before his head descends and his lips find mine.

"They're making out again!" I hear Barney shout and end the kiss with Max to watch him walk into the apartment.

"Of course, they are. They're probably going to christen the sofa before the day's over," Sid adds as he walks by carrying a box.

"Five bucks says the kid cockblocks them."

I bury my head in Max's shoulder at Lenny's words. "And I thought raising Ollie was work. Now, I've got four more kids to deal with."

"At least we're potty trained," Wally says as he plops down on the sofa next to us.

I giggle. I came to this city to escape my home and discovered the home and family I always wished I had. I cuddle deeper into Max. Yeah, this is home.

Chapter 35

I hate it when everyone asks me what's for dinner just because I'm the mom.

THANKSGIVING

I stand back and observe the table I decorated for our family Thanksgiving lunch. It's a big table with room for all of Max's brothers and Hailey and her friends and their husbands. The only people missing are Valerie and my parents. Valerie's working, and my parents can't afford to visit for both Thanksgiving and Christmas. I gave Ollie the choice, and he asked for them to come for Christmas.

Max wraps an arm around me. "Missing your parents?"

In the weeks since we've lived together, he's learned to read me like an open book. It's infuriating at times and comforting at others. "Yeah. My mom bakes the best sweet potato pie you'll ever eat."

Pepper barks and then comes barreling into the room with Ollie chasing after her. "I thought you were going to put her in her kennel."

"She got away from me," he yells as he runs past. Max takes one step and picks the puppy off the ground.

"Put her in her kennel," he orders as he hands Ollie the dog.

"Yeah, yeah," Ollie says as he carries the squirming puppy out of the room.

"Still happy you bought my son's love with a dog?" Pepper has not only peed and pooped nearly daily in his apartment, but she's also destroyed several pillows and gnawed on the corner of his coffee table.

"I'd do it all over again," he whispers before claiming my lips.

"Oh god," Phoebe squeaks. "They're making out. Someone tell them to stop."

Ryker grunts. "Princess."

"Saying Princess is not an answer, big guy."

"We're done," I shout.

"Not done. Taking a break," Max whispers in my ear, and I shiver.

"Stop being sexy, Pops," Phoebe rants.

"Pops is being sexy? Where?" Suzie pushes past them. Grayson takes her hand and slows her down.

"Whoa, momma. Be careful." He helps her down the two steps into the bar.

She takes off her winter coat and hands it to him. "Oh my!" I cry when I see she's sporting the cutest little baby bump.

She twists and turns as if she's modeling. "She's growing like crazy," she says as she rubs her bump.

"The baby is a boy," Grayson insists.

"Are we arguing about the baby's sex again?" Hailey asks as she walks in.

"Fifty bucks says it's a boy," Lenny says from behind Hailey.

"I'll take your bet!" Suzie announces.

Grayson growls. "You are not betting on the sex of our child."

"Why not? You afraid to lose, Soldier?" Lenny goads him.

"What's going on? Why is there a hold up at the door?" My eyes widen when I hear the question. I know that voice!

I whirl on Max. "You didn't!"

He shrugs, but his cheeks darken and give him away. I give him a quick, hard kiss before rushing to the door.

"Mom! Dad!"

The crowd parts, and there they stand. I rush to my mom and throw my arms around her. Pressure builds behind my eyes, but I sniff to stop the tears from falling. I won't ruin the day by crying. My dad takes my elbow and steers us away from the doorway.

I squeeze my mom one last time before releasing her. I take my dad's hand and haul him further into the room. "Everyone, these are my parents – Cora and Martin Tilly."

I motion to Max. "This is Max."

Max shakes my dad's hand. "We spoke on the phone. Nice to meet you in person."

My mom ignores his hand and flings herself into his arms. "I'm glad my stubborn daughter finally found a man worthy of her."

"I am not stubborn."

Sid laughs as he shuts the door behind him and Mary Ann. "Sure, you aren't."

Mary Ann slaps his arm. "It takes one to know one."

"Grandma! Grandpa!" Ollie screams and runs full tilt toward them and throws himself at them.

While I'm watching Ollie hug his grandparents, the door bangs open.

"This is not over," Wally grumbles at Chrissie.

She snorts. "This is totally over," she dismisses him before smiling my way. "I brought my green bean casserole."

I motion for her to follow me to the kitchen. "What's going on with you and Wally?"

"Nothing. He's a dick is all."

"Do you need us to talk to him?"

"Talk to him," Suzie says as she sticks her head into the kitchen. "Let's prank him."

Hailey and Phoebe look over her shoulder and nod in agreement. Chrissie dismisses their concern with a wave of her hand. "I got this. Wally doesn't have a clue who he's up against."

Uh oh. She said the wrong thing. Now, Suzie is practically salivating to find out what's going on. "Come on. Who's going to help me take the food out?" I ask to distract them.

Grayson arrives and nabs Suzie's hand. "Sorry, pregnant lady is not allowed to carry anything."

Hailey snorts. "I think you mean klutzy lady."

"Hey!" Whatever retort Suzie was going to make is muffled when Grayson places his hand on her mouth and drags her away.

"You know he's not going to let her lift a finger until she pops out his baby," Hailey remarks.

"Good for him," I say. Suzie deserves a man who treats her like she's precious while she's carrying his baby. Hell, every pregnant woman deserves to be treated like a princess.

Hailey, Phoebe, and Chrissie help me take the massive amounts of food out to the table while the guys add another two seats and Max gets everyone a drink. Meanwhile, Ollie is showing my parents around the pub.

"As soon as I'm sixteen, I'm going to start working here," he says.

I slam the dish of stuffing I'm holding onto the table. "You're going to do what?"

"Work here. Hailey said she worked here from the time she was sixteen."

Max arrives and squeezes my neck. "Let's discuss this later, shall we?"

"Why later?" Barney asks. "It's not Thanksgiving unless someone's having a fight."

I whirl on him. "I'll show you a fight."

"Whoa!" He holds up his hands. "Mama Bear is in the house." He snickers. "What do you call—"

I slap a hand over his mouth. "No. No dirty jokes in front of my parents and son."

My mom laughs. "Quite the family you've made here, Faith."

My dad wraps an arm around my waist. "You always did want brothers."

"Yeah, well. I was an idiot."

Max raises his voice to be heard above the crowd, "Come on, everyone. Find your seats. Let's eat while it's hot."

Before we can take our places, the door bangs open again. "What now?"

"What now? Is that any way to greet your favorite person in the world?"

I screech when I see Valerie standing in the entryway with her hands on her hips. I rush to her and nearly take her down when I throw myself into her arms. "I thought you couldn't make it?" I ask after I release her.

She snorts. "As if those lawyers were going to keep me from celebrating Thanksgiving with my family. Where's my boy?"

Ollie shuffles over. "Hi, Valerie." She swoops him into her arms.

After she sets Ollie down, I take her arm and twirl her toward the group of people watching us. "This is my friend Valerie. Valerie, this is everyone."

Barney saunters over, and I groan. "Here I am. What are your other two wishes?"

Valerie winks at him. "You're a bit skinny, but I guess you'll do."

Barney pales. "Skinny? I'll do?"

I laugh and lead her away before she attacks him. Valerie is not shy about her sexuality at all. If she sees someone she likes – and guessing from the way she's licking her lips while gazing at Barney, she likes what she sees – she goes for it.

Valerie hugs my parents in greeting before I introduce her to everyone else. And then, finally, we can take our seats. I watch as Valerie takes the seat next to Barney who gulps as she sits down. This is going to be fun!

Max pours me a glass of champagne and tilts his head toward my plate. My brow wrinkles but I look down to see my plate is no longer empty.

"Why is there a chocolate bar on my plate?" I survey the other place settings, but no one else has a chocolate bar.

"Open it, Ma."

"What's going on here?" I ask the group, but everyone looks away. "I shouldn't ruin my appetite with chocolate."

Ollie groans. "Not every moment is a teaching moment."

When everyone laughs, I give in and pick up the candy bar. I unwrap the bar and gasp at the words I find engraved into the chocolate. *Marry me?*

I search the room for Max and find him on his knee next to me. "Will you marry me, Faith Bakker?"

I purse my lips. "Seriously? That's it? No heartfelt speech? No romance?"

"Told you!" Ollie says.

"Faith Bakker, you captured my heart the minute you walked into this room looking for a job and ignored Sid's clichéd attempt to pick you up."

"Hey!" Mary Ann cries.

"You were terrified, but you straightened your back and asked me for a job. I knew then you were a strong woman I wanted to get to know. And every little thing I've learned about you since then has strengthened my awe of you. It took me fifty-six years, but I've finally found the woman who holds my heart in her hands."

Tears sting my eyes, and I sniff to keep them from falling. "You're pretty good at this romance stuff."

"What do you say? You want to become an official member of this family?"

"Say yes, Faith," Hailey shouts.

"Did you ask my dad for permission first?" I ask because I'm not above a bit of teasing.

He rolls his eyes. "Why do you think your parents are here?"

"I approve. This one seems to have his head screwed on straight, unlike Silas." Dad coughs and looks at Ollie. "No offense to your dad, Oliver."

"Please tell me someone is recording this," Mary Ann says. "This is going to get like two gazillion hits."

Hailey holds up her phone. "I got it!"

"Will you put me out of my misery now? We both know you're going to say yes anyway."

I glare at Max. "Maybe I need some time to think about it."

"Ma," Ollie whines. "Stop teasing Pops."

"I guess if my son approves..."

Max whoops and springs to his feet. He lifts me out of my chair and whirls me around. I slap his shoulders. "Put me down. I want to see my ring."

"What if I didn't get you a ring yet?"

As if he wouldn't have a ring. "Then, you're going to run out and buy me one and do the entire proposal again."

He winks and removes a black velvet, jewelry box from his pocket. "Good thing I have a ring then."

He slips the ring on my finger, and I stare at it. An extremely large round solitaire sits on a white gold band covered in diamonds. "You're crazy. This diamond borders on obnoxious."

Hailey joins us. "Pops never does things small." She pulls me into a hug. "Congrats, stepmom."

Oh lord, I'm a stepmom. "Be good or I won't let you go to the ball."

Ollie shuffles over to us. "Congrats, Ma." He looks up and cringes. "She's got the I'm going to suffocate you look again."

I don't deny it. I hug him up tight and sway side to side with him. "You okay with this?"

"Yeah," he says as he squirms until I let him go. "Actually, I have a question."

"Go for it."

"Um, it's a question for Pops."

Max steps closer. "What is it, son?"

Ollie plays with the buttons of his shirt. "Well, I was wondering. Since you're marrying my mom and all. And you call me son anyway. And Hailey calls me her stepbrother. Then, maybe it would be an idea if you like… make it official."

Max swallows before asking, "You want me to adopt you?"

Ollie's face pinkens. "Only if you want to, of course."

Max looks at me, but I've lost the ability to speak. I'm too busy melting into a gooey puddle of love. Ollie loves the man I'm in love with. I couldn't ask for a better gift. I don't bother trying to stop the tears forming in my eyes from rolling down my cheeks.

"And if Hailey's okay with it, too."

"I'd be honored for you to be a part of my family," Hailey says and squeezes his shoulder.

"It's settled, then. I'm marrying your mom and adopting you." Max sniffs and I see him wipe a tear away. "I don't know how I got this lucky."

He doesn't know how *he* got this lucky? I'm the one who's lucky.

"Can we eat now?" Barney whines. "I'm starving."

"I've got something you can eat," Valerie whisper-shouts.

I laugh and join my family for Thanksgiving. I have a lot to be thankful for this year and for the rest of my life. Take that, universe. This single mom doesn't need to keep score any longer.

D. E. Haggerty
Love and Laughter in Every Chapter

About the Author

D.E. Haggerty is an American who has spent the majority of her adult life abroad. She has lived in Istanbul, various places throughout Germany, and currently finds herself in The Hague. She has been a military policewoman, a lawyer, a B&B owner/operator and now a writer.